CORPORATE ASSETS

SANDI LYNN

SANDI LYNN ROMANCE, LLC

Corporate Assets

Copyright © 2016 Sandi Lynn Romance, LLC

All rights reserved. No part of this publication may be reproduced, distributed, or transmitted in any form or by any means, including photocopying, recording, or other electronic or mechanical methods without the prior written permission of the publisher.
This is a work of fiction. Names, characters, places and incidents are the products of the author's imagination or are used factitiously. Any resemblance to actual events, locales, or persons, living or dead, is entirely coincidental.

❦ Created with Vellum

MISSION STATEMENT

Sandi Lynn Romance

Providing readers with romance novels that will whisk them away to another world and from the daily grind of life – one book at a time.

CHAPTER 1

Fiona

"Hey, babe. I have to cancel our dinner plans for tonight. Emergency at the office and I have to work late. I'll make it up to you. Love you to pieces."

I sat on the edge of my bed, staring at the text message that enraged me. Emergency at the office, my ass. Getting up from my bed, I walked over to my laptop, and after a few keystrokes, I was in. In John's phone account where I had access to all his text messages.

"Hey, baby. We're on for tonight. I'll pick you up at seven. Make sure to wear something extra sexy and no panties. While we're sitting at the blackjack table, I want to feel how wet you get when my fingers touch that beautiful pussy of yours."

"You're a dirty man, John, and I can't wait. You know I always wear something extra sexy for my man."

"I'm already getting hard just thinking about you."

Her man? Are you fucking kidding me? I knew that bastard was cheating on me. A woman's intuition is never wrong. Late nights at the office, multiple cancellation of dates, way too many out of town business trips, and one too many phone calls he had to excuse himself for. Picking up my phone, I dialed my best friend, Lydia.

"Hello," she answered.

"I need you to come over. We're going out tonight."

"Where? I thought you had dinner plans with John."

"He has an emergency at the office and has to work late. Or should I say, he has an emergency at the casino with some whore who called him 'her' man."

"Shit, Fiona. Seriously?"

"Yes. I'll explain when you get here. Do you still have those wigs we wore to that Halloween party two years ago?"

"Yeah. Why?"

"We're going to need them."

She squealed. "Sounds like fun. I'm on my way."

Lydia Jones and I met in our freshman year at UCLA when we were paired up as roommates. The minute we met, we instantly became best friends and were always there to protect each other. It was rare that we weren't together and everyone knew us as the "dorm twins," meaning that we looked alike. Same height, same long blonde hair, and same petite frame. The only difference was her eyes were brown and mine were blue. We even worked for the same company. Right before graduating college, the two of us were offered positions at Steiner & Richards Marketing Firm.

*A*fter creating the perfect smoky eye and sweeping a blush called "Obsessed" across my cheeks, I stained my lips with a color called Scarlet Red.

"So, how exactly are we going to do this?" Lydia asked.

"We're going to go in and watch."

"The casino is huge, Fiona. How are we going to find him?"

"He'll be sitting at the same blackjack table he always does." I placed the short, bob-styled, jet-black wig on my head and smiled.

After getting into my short, black, body-hugging, low cut dress, I slipped my feet into the black stiletto heels I had been dying to wear since I bought them.

"Damn. You look hot as fuck." Lydia smiled. "I don't even recognize you. Especially with all that makeup."

"Thanks. You look hot too and you look good as a brunette. I just need to do one last thing before we go." I grabbed my phone and sent John a text message.

"I miss you already, baby. Don't work too hard. Can you come by in the morning?"

"I miss you too. Probably not, baby. God knows how late I'll be here at the office tonight. It's just one problem after another. Don't worry that pretty little head of yours. I'll make it up to you. Remember, I love you to pieces."

"My bed will be lonely tonight without you in it."

"I'll be lonely tonight without you. I have to go. TTYL."

Asshole.

"Let's go!" I exclaimed as I grabbed the black duffle bag from the floor and my clutch.

"What's in the bag?" Lydia asked with concern.

"You'll see." I smiled.

John and I had been together for a little over a year. We met right after my mother passed away and I needed a shoulder to cry on. I was vulnerable, he was there, and it seemed to work. Did I really love him? Yes. Was I in love with him? Not so sure, but I did like being with him and I wouldn't tolerate being lied to and cheated on. If he wanted to be with someone else, all he had to do was tell me, and now, he was going to pay for his little indiscretion.

Light waves of smoke streamed through the air. The music was loud, but not loud enough to drown out the bells and whistles that radiated from the slot machines. Boisterous voices could be heard throughout. Some patrons were winning tons of cash, while others screamed at their losses.

"Are you sure you know which table he's at?" Lydia asked.

"Follow me." I led her over to the bar, where luckily, two stools were available. Taking a seat, I signaled for the bartender.

His eyes swept over me and diverted their attention straight to my cleavage as a smile crossed his lips.

"What can I get you, darling?"

"I'll have a scotch on the rocks. Make it a double. I'm feeling lucky tonight." I winked.

"And for you?" He smiled at Lydia.

"I'll have a gin and tonic." She batted her lashes over her brown eyes. "So, why are we sitting here?"

"Because he's right over there." I pointed to the blackjack table across from the bar where John sat next to a woman with long red hair.

As I sipped on my scotch, I studied them. The small kisses they stole and the way his hand slipped under her silvery dress. The redhead got up from her seat and headed towards the restrooms.

"I'll be right back," I spoke as I stood up.

"You're not going to assault her, are you?" Lydia asked.

"No." I smiled.

Following her into the restroom, I pretended to touch up my makeup until she came out from the stall.

"It's pretty busy in here tonight," I spoke.

"Yeah. It is." She smiled as she washed her hands.

Red hair, green eyes, five foot four without her heels on, and a tiny frame. I'd admit she was pretty.

"Are you winning tonight?" I asked.

"I'm not, but my boyfriend is. He always seems to win every time we come here."

"You come here often?"

"About twice a week. John loves to gamble." She pulled a tube of lipstick out from her purse.

"This is my first time here. It's a girls' night out. My boyfriend and I just broke up." I spoke with a fake sadness as I looked down.

"Aw, I'm sorry. How long were you together?"

"A year. How long have you been with your boyfriend?"

"Let's see. Six months." She smacked her lips together after applying her lipstick. "May I ask why you broke up?"

"He cheated on me." I sniffled as I began to fake a cry.

"Aw, sweetie. I'm sorry. Men are idiots. You know what? You're a good person. That much I can tell and he didn't deserve you."

"Thank you. I appreciate it." I pretended to dab my eye with a tissue. "I'm sure your boyfriend would never do that to you."

A small smile crossed her lips. "No. John is the sweetest, most caring, generous, and loving man I have ever met. We are so in love."

The anger I had been controlling since I read his text message was surfacing, and any minute, it was about to be released.

"I'm happy for you. Make sure you hold on to him."

"Oh, I definitely will. Take care, sweetie, and don't let your ex ruin your night. You go out there and have a shitload of fun."

"I totally intend to." I smiled slyly.

After she left the bathroom, I waited behind for a few moments until it was clear. Six months? We'd only been dating six months before he started a relationship with her. That little motherfucker. The clicking of my heels echoed as I walked to the door. Making my way back to the bar, I noticed a man sitting in my seat. Lydia shrugged as she saw me coming.

"Excuse me. I was sitting here."

The man turned around and I swallowed hard. Short brown hair that sported a touch of gold highlights, perfectly straight nose, captivating green eyes that held you in a trance when you looked into them, perfectly shaped lips, high cheekbones, and the perfect amount of stubble across his jawline.

The corners of his mouth curved up into a smile as his eyes stared into mine.

"I'm sorry. I didn't know anyone was sitting here. Let me buy you a drink to apologize."

Shit. The word "no" wouldn't escape my mouth. I couldn't let anyone or anything distract me from my mission tonight.

"Thank you, but no," I finally managed to speak.

"No?" His brow arched.

Something told me this man wasn't used to hearing that word.

"All I need you to do is kindly remove yourself from my seat."

"I will after you tell me what you're drinking tonight." He smirked.

I studied him for a moment. Probably longer than I should have.

But it couldn't be helped. My eyes had never seen such sexiness before, and for a brief moment, they were happy.

"I'm curious. Has a woman ever said no to you before?" I asked.

"No. They haven't. That word doesn't exist around me."

Oh boy. This guy was a total douchebag.

"Then let me be your first. The answer is no. I'm not telling you what I'm drinking and you're not buying me a drink. But thank you for the offer." I smiled politely.

His gorgeous eyes narrowed at me as he cocked his head.

"Then I'm not getting up."

Now he was really pissing me off, drop dead sexy or not. I glanced over at John and the redhead sitting at the Blackjack table. His hand was all the way up her dress as he leaned over and brushed his mouth against hers.

"That's fine. We're leaving anyway." I grabbed hold of Lydia's hand and pulled her behind me.

CHAPTER 2

Fiona

"Holy shit, Fiona. What the hell just happened back there? Did you see the way he looked at you? It looked like he was eye raping you and wanted to devour you."

"Fuck him."

"I sure would and I would've let him buy me a drink."

"We aren't here to pick up guys, Lydia. Or have you forgotten?"

"Oh yeah. How did it go in the bathroom? I was getting worried."

"Apparently, they've been dating for the last six months." My feet hit the pavement as the warm air blew across my face.

"What? You've only been dating for a year."

"No shit."

"So now what?" she asked as she ran to keep up with me.

"To your car."

We climbed into her Ford Escape. She gripped the steering wheel as she stared at me while I took the black bag from the back seat.

"His car is in this parking garage somewhere." I casually smiled.

"Oh shit, Fiona. What are you going to do?"

"You'll see. Just drive. There it is." I pointed.

Second level. His brand new Audi R8 V10. Owned for approximately two weeks. He had it parked sideways, taking up two spaces so no one could park next to him. It was his baby and every time he got out of it, he would wipe it down with a cloth.

"Just keep driving," I spoke as I looked up at the security camera in the corner.

"To where?"

"There's a car pulling out over there." I pointed. "Pull in and then I'm going to need you to do me a favor. I need you to go back inside the casino and go to security. Distract them. Tell them that your car was parked on the first level and when you went to leave the casino you noticed it was gone. Act like a neurotic and desperate woman and get them down to the first level to check it out. I'll text you when I'm ready to be picked up."

"Then what do I say?"

"Just tell them that you made a mistake and you actually parked on the third level. Act like the blonde you are, my friend." I smirked.

"This better work."

"It will. Trust me. I need you to text me when you get the guard away from the monitor."

Holding my phone in my hand, I patiently waited for Lydia's text. This was the last thing I needed in my life. How could he carry on two relationships? I would have noticed something was up sooner if I wasn't knee deep in trying to get that promotion at work. After about ten minutes, a text from Lydia came through.

"He's with me and away from the monitor. He's really hot, by the way."

Rolling my eyes, I grabbed the can of black spray paint, walked up to the camera with my head down, and sprayed the lens black. Walking back over to Lydia's car, I grabbed my bag and set it down next to John's car. Taking out the wooden baseball bat, I began to smash each headlight. But I wouldn't stop there.

"This is for twelve months of nothing." I smashed the driver's side window. "And for all the 'I love yous' that you didn't mean." I smashed out the back window. Reaching down into the bag, I pulled out a large jackknife and slashed all four tires. As I dragged the knife along the doors of his sport red Audi R8, I noticed a black limo slowly pulling up. That was my cue to go. After slashing his leather seat, I placed the bat and the knife back into the bag and picked it up. Placing my hand on my head, I pulled off my wig, and as I turned to throw it in the trash can, my eyes locked with Dreamy Eyes from the bar. The corners of his mouth curved upwards as he stared at me and I threw the bag over my shoulder and casually walked away.

Nathan

What the fuck was she doing? I couldn't believe my eyes as we drove on the second level of the parking garage and I saw that gorgeous woman from the bar beating the hell out of someone's car. It was quite a turn on, actually. Brunettes weren't my thing, but her. She was different. The moment I turned around and saw those baby blue eyes staring at me, I instantly became intrigued. And that body. Fuck. Toned, slender, long legs that I wanted wrapped around my waist and beautiful perky tits that were pushed up by the tight-fitting dress she wore. Plump red lips that would satisfy me while they were wrapped around my hard cock. I'd say she stood about five foot seven without the stilettos she was wearing with an incredible hour-glass figure. She definitely had piqued my interest. An interest that I wanted to invest in until she told me no and walked away. Then, the parking garage. I gasped and sat in shock as she tore the wig from her head and strands of long blonde hair came falling down. My cock immediately rose when she turned and those beautiful blue eyes stared straight at me. I needed to know who she was and why she destroyed that car.

By the time I told Jason to step on it, she was gone. Gone without a trace. Damn it.

"Forget about her, Nathan," Jason, my driver spoke. "Obviously, she's crazy. Look what she did to that car."

"I like crazy." I smiled.

As soon as I got home, I poured myself a drink and took a seat on the patio. I couldn't get her out of my head. First she said no to me and then she went and trashed somebody's poor car. Must have been a boyfriend or something. From what I saw, she had the look of revenge. I did catch her glancing over at a blackjack table while I was trying to convince her to let me buy her a drink. And why the wig? She was obviously trying to hide herself. She was someone I needed to quickly put to rest. I'd never know who she was or where she came from. Easier said than done. Her face, her eyes, and the word no would be with me for a long time.

CHAPTER 3

Fiona

The alarm went off sharply at five-thirty a.m. Shutting it off, I looked at my phone to see if I had any messages from John. I didn't. I expected he would have called me last night when he found his precious baby had been destroyed. But I was sure he was being consoled all night by the redhead. Stumbling out of bed, I popped a k-cup in the Keurig and watched as it streamed into the cup. The thought had crossed my mind that John was going to have to come up with a pretty hefty lie to cover his tracks from last night.

As I stepped out of the shower, there was a knock at my door. A smile crossed my face because I knew it was John.

"John. What are you doing here? You said you couldn't stop by this morning,"

"You're never going to fucking believe what happened last night." He came darting in.

"What?"

"Someone vandalized my car," he spoke in anger and I could see the vein throbbing in his neck.

"What?!" I exclaimed. "At the office?"

"Umm. Yeah. At the office."

"Oh my God. How bad is it?"

"Really bad, Fiona. They cut all my tires. Smashed the windshield, back window, headlights, tore up my leather seats, and scratched the paint with something really sharp. Right down to the metal. FUCK!" he yelled.

"Why didn't you call me last night?"

He paced around my condo, back and forth with his hands tightly tucked into his pant pockets.

"Because it was too late and there wasn't anything you could do. Who the fuck would do this?"

"Well, if it happened at the office, there are security cameras. Can't you check them?"

A few moments of silence filled the room.

"Apparently, the cameras weren't working." He sighed.

"Did you call the police?"

"I sure did. But without any witnesses or security footage, there isn't anything they can do. You know how much that car meant to me."

Walking over to where he was standing, I shuddered as I wrapped my arms around him.

"I'm sorry, John. I know how hard this must be for you." I buried my face in his neck as a small smile crossed my lips. "I just can't believe it happened at your office. Were any other cars vandalized?"

He broke our embrace and continued to pace around the room.

"No. Only mine. The weird thing is nothing was stolen out of the car. It's like whoever did it, did it for the thrill of it or something."

"Hmm. That's strange." I picked up my coffee cup and took a sip from it. "Did you piss someone off?"

"Not that I know of."

"Listen, I need to get ready for work now." I walked over and ran my finger down his shirt. "Are you going to take me out tonight to make up for last night?"

"I have a meeting tonight with a potential client."

"How about after?"

"I don't know how long it's going to run. We'll do something tomorrow night. Okay?" He brushed his lips against mine.

I pulled away.

"Sure. Unless another meeting comes up." I walked away.

"Fiona." John came after me. "I love you, baby. I love you so much and I don't need you being mad at me. It's been a shitty night and today isn't going to be any better." He lightly grabbed my arm.

I turned and stared into his lying eyes, not speaking a word.

"You know how much I love being with you and it kills me that I always have to work late. I promise to make it up to you. Trust me."

Trust him? I silently laughed to myself. Trusting him or any man wasn't in me.

"I do trust you." I gently smiled.

"There's my baby's smile." His thumb touched my lips. "Have a good day at work. I'll call you later, okay?"

"Okay." I nodded.

As soon as he left, I grabbed a pillow from the couch and placed it over my face, screaming into it as loud as I could. How could he lie to my face like that? He had no soul and I wasn't standing for it any longer.

※

Walking through the doors of Steiner and Richards Marketing firm, I took the elevator up to my office where I found Lydia sitting in the seat across from my desk.

"Good morning." I smiled as I handed her a cup of coffee I picked up from Starbucks.

"Morning. Did you hear from him?"

"Yep. He came crying to me this morning about his precious car. Even told me that it happened at the office and the security cameras weren't working."

"Asshole." She grinned.

"Then he went on to say how he couldn't take me out tonight, but he promises tomorrow night and to trust him."

"Ugh. Total douchebag. What are you going to do?"

"Break up with him."

"I would hope so. When?"

"Today."

"How?"

"I haven't figured that out yet. But I will." I winked.

"Hey, Fiona, I need to see you in my office," my boss, Kevin, spoke.

"I'll be right there, Kevin." I smiled.

Despite John ruining my morning, I was happy because today was the day that the promotion to marketing manager was mine. I'd been working my ass off for the past five years, working my way up to this very position.

"Good luck. We'll have to go and celebrate tonight." Lydia smiled.

"Thanks. I'll talk to you later." I got up from my desk and headed into Kevin's office.

CHAPTER 4

Fiona

"Have a seat, Fiona," Kevin spoke as he leaned back in his chair. "I want to give you a heads up. Bryce is giving the promotion to Celia. I'm sorry."

Did I just hear him correctly?

"What?" I cocked my head in disbelief.

"I'm sorry. It's out of my hands. Trust me, I did everything I could."

"I'm sorry?" I shook my head. "Celia? The woman who has less experience than me? The woman who screwed up so badly on the Nike account that I saved and kept them from going to another marketing firm?"

"I know this is hard. Again, I'm sorry."

"I knew that little whore was sleeping with him." I got up in a rage. "I bet his wife doesn't know, does she?" I glared at Kevin.

"No." He shook his head as he looked down. "Bryce is making the announcement this afternoon. I didn't want you blindsided. The promotion should have been yours, Fiona, but it's his company and I did my best."

Rage consumed me. Even more rage than John's other girlfriend. The funny part was that Celia was also a redhead. Screwed over twice by redheads. Nice. This wasn't Kevin's fault. I knew he had done everything he could, and I deserved that promotion. The air in the room was thick and my breathing suddenly became restricted. The angrier I became, the harder it was to breathe.

"Calm down, Fiona." He handed me a glass of vodka. "I know it isn't fair."

"I can't work here anymore, Kevin. I'm done."

"You don't mean that. You're one of the best account executives we have. Don't do something stupid in the heat of the moment."

"Heat of the moment? This is my future. I'll be damned if I'm going to let some whore walk around here gloating because she slept her way to the top. That was my promotion, Kevin." I pointed my finger at him.

"I know." He clasped my shoulders. "There will be other promotions. If you quit and go somewhere else, you'll have to start all over and you're too smart for that. Listen, just calm down, let it go, and keep working like you do. I promise in the end, it'll pay off."

"Fine." I handed him the empty glass and walked back to my office, telling my secretary, Lynn, that under no circumstances was I to be bothered.

As I sat at my desk, the tears started to fall. Taking my hand and wiping them away, I thought about how much my life sucked. This wasn't fair. The promotion, John, none of it. I'd been cheated on and lied to by a person who claimed to love me and I'd lost my future because of a man who couldn't keep his dick in his pants. The more I thought about it, the more the anger ripped through me. Fuck him!

I got up from my desk, flung my office door open, and took the elevator up to Bryce's office.

"Is he in there?" I scowled at his secretary.

"Yes. But he's—"

Hearing the word "yes" was all I needed as I opened his door and stepped inside, closing it behind me.

"I have to call you back, sweetheart. Someone just walked in. Fiona?" He set down his phone.

"That promotion was mine, Bryce!"

He sighed. "I'm sorry, Fiona. Celia—"

"Celia sucks your dick and that's the only reason she got the promotion over me!" I shouted.

"For god sakes, keep your voice down. What can I do? You want a raise? It's yours."

"I wanted that promotion." I pointed at him.

"I'm sorry, Fiona. I really am."

"My ass you are. I quit, Bryce." I walked towards the door.

"If you walk out on me now, don't think that I'll be giving you any good recommendations for another job."

Slowly turning around, my eyes burned into his. "I wonder what your wife will say when she finds out about Celia?"

"You wouldn't dare," he growled.

"Oh, I would. Trust me. I like to call it my right as a woman to inform another that she's being cheated on by her douchebag husband. It's called girl code. So what were you saying again about recommendations?"

"I'll make sure you get one of the best ones."

"That's what I thought you said." I stormed out of his office.

*

As soon as I got home, I immediately changed into my pajamas, took a pint of ice cream from the freezer, grabbed a bottle of wine, and planted myself on the couch. Now that I'd gone and quit my job, it was time to take care of my relationship. Picking up my phone, I sent a text message to John.

"I don't think we should see each other anymore, so I'm breaking up with you."

I patiently waited for a response.

"What? Fiona, stop joking. I'm really busy today."

"I'm not joking, John. I'm done with our relationship."

"What the fuck! Why?"

If I told him I found out about his other girlfriend, he'd know I was the one who trashed his car.

"Because I realized that you don't have time for me. I'm not a priority in your life."

"Baby, I'll come over after work and we'll talk about this. Of course you are a priority."

"No, John, I'm not. It's over."

"Is that how you really feel?"

"Yes. I have never felt so strong about anything in my life."

"Fine. It's over. Good riddance, Fiona."

"Good riddance, John."

Letting out a sigh, I set my phone down and took a large bite of ice cream.

CHAPTER 5

Nathan

"You were amazing." Claudia smiled as she ran her finger down my chest.

"Thanks." I climbed out of her bed and pulled on my pants.

"Where are you going?"

"We fucked and I'm done. I'm going home."

"I thought you were staying the night!" she pouted.

"Listen, sweetheart, I know you're new to this with me, but let's get one thing straight. I don't spend the night with the women I have sex with." I buttoned up my shirt.

"Ever?"

"Never." I smiled.

"So you used me?" she snapped.

"I wouldn't say that. You wanted me to fuck you, so I did. And if we're going to continue to do this, then you have to understand that I will never stay."

"You're just a real unromantic asshole."

"Romance isn't my thing, and as for being an asshole, I admit that I can be. So I'm not offended."

"Get out, Nathan, and don't call me." She brought her knees up to her chest.

"Suit yourself, sweetheart. There are plenty of women out there who understand." I headed towards the door. "One question before I leave. What gave you the impression that I was a romantic kind of guy?"

She stared at me for a moment. "I guess you never did."

"Exactly." I winked. "So shame on you for thinking that I was."

Climbing into the limo, I sighed, and Jason looked at me through the rearview mirror.

"She wanted you to stay?" he asked.

"Yep. She told me not to call her."

He laughed. "And another one bites the dust."

"No big deal. She wasn't that good anyway."

"You are the true definition of a Casanova, my friend."

*

Fiona

I hadn't left my house in over two weeks and it was in shambles.

"You really need to get your life together. It's been two weeks. Have you even started looking for a new job?" Lydia asked as she started to clean up the two weeks' worth of mess.

"There's something I need to tell you," I spoke with seriousness. "And I'm not sure how to."

She set down the glasses and took a seat next to me.

"What?"

"I got a new job and it's in New York. I start next week."

"When did that happen?" she asked.

"Today. I did a skype interview with a marketing company a few days ago and yesterday, I had a second interview. Today, they called and said that my recommendation from Bryce was stellar and they were excited to have me on board."

Lydia reached over and placed her hand on mine.

"I don't want you to go. You're my best friend. We've been together since freshman year of college."

"I know, sweetie. But I feel like I need a new start. It's a really good job and I'm not starting at the bottom."

Suddenly, my phone rang.

"That's weird. It's my step-monster. Why the hell would she be calling? Hello," I answered.

"Fiona." She sniffled. "Your father passed away."

I sat there in shock, unable to speak as my heart started pounding rapidly.

"Oh my God! How?" Tears formed in my eyes and my body began to shake.

"He had a massive heart attack. I'm at the hospital now."

"I'm on my way."

Setting my phone down, I looked at Lydia. "My father just died."

※

After the funeral, I made a call to the company in New York to let them know that I wouldn't be able to start for a couple of more weeks due to the death of my father. They were very understanding and told me to take as much time as I needed. As much as Rachel and I didn't get along, I couldn't just leave her to clean out my father's things on her own.

"Robbie called and needs us to come into his office tomorrow. He said there's something he needs to discuss about your father's company," she spoke.

"What about it?"

"I don't know. Could you spend the night again? I really don't want to be alone." She began to cry.

"Yeah. I'll stay. That way, we can go together tomorrow and then I'll help you go through Dad's things before I leave for New York."

"Thank you, Fiona. Listen, I know we never got along, but your dad would want us to do this together."

I sighed. "He would. I think I'm going to head up to bed. It's been a long past couple of days and I'm exhausted."

"Me too." She blew her nose.

The truth was, Rachel and I didn't get along because she was responsible for the breakup of my parents' marriage. Which also led to the distance that had grown between me and my father. They met ten years ago when I was eighteen when they were involved in a little fender bender at a stop light. They exchanged numbers, settled with the insurance company, and shortly after, a relationship formed. My father told my mother about Rachel a month after they started dating. She had quickly become the most important thing in his life. He left my mother devastated, I went off to college, and he continued on as if he did nothing wrong. We barely spoke during my college years. The plan had always been since I was a little girl that I would go to college, get my MBA, and go to work for his company, Winslow Wines. But that changed when he married Rachel because I no longer wanted anything to do with him or his company. It wasn't until two years ago that we started to reconnect when my mother was diagnosed with breast cancer, which she lost her battle to over a year ago. I never thought in a million years that I'd lose both my parents in such a short amount of time.

The next morning, Rachel and I headed to Robbie's office at Winslow Wines. He was my mother's brother, my uncle, and also the financial manager for the company ever since the doors first opened.

"Hi, Uncle Robbie." I smiled as I gave him a hug.

"Hi, Fiona. Rachel. Please have a seat. You know, Devin, your father's lawyer."

"Hello, Devin." I nodded.

"What's this about?" Rachel asked.

Devin opened a large brown envelope and took out a stack of papers.

"This is your father's Will pertaining to the company. To be read three days after he was put to rest." He cleared his throat. "Upon my death, my company, Winslow Wines, shall be given to my only child,

Fiona Rose Winslow, to oversee and run to the best of her ability and to keep the family company for generations to come."

"What?!" I exclaimed. "No. I'm moving to New York."

"This is what your father wanted, Fiona," my Uncle Robbie spoke. "If he didn't think you could do it, he wouldn't have put you in charge of something he built from nothing."

"You have got to be kidding me." I got up from my chair and paced around the office. "I don't know the first thing about running a company."

"I'll be here to help you," Uncle Robbie spoke.

"And what about the board of directors? Do you think they're going to stand for this?"

"It doesn't matter," Devin spoke. "Your father was the majority shareholder, which has been passed on to you. They have no choice but to back you."

"And if I don't want it?"

"Then you can sell your shares, the company, and destroy everything your father worked so hard to build."

CHAPTER 6

Fiona

Guilt. Pure guilt. That was what they were throwing at me. What the hell did I know about running a company? What if I failed and then I'd have to live with the guilt for letting my father down for the rest of my life. Was this something I could do? Hell if I knew. I was business smart. I always had been and I knew that it broke my father's heart when I refused to come work for him. But I was angry. Angry that he cheated on my mother, divorced her, destroyed our family, and married Rachel. The best way I could handle my anger was to distance myself from him. It was what I did. But then my mother was diagnosed with breast cancer and I had to turn to him. He was there for me, helping me and my mom. He supported me through it all. He was the strength I needed to get through it when I had nobody else, and he was there for me when she died.

"Okay." I sighed. "Where do I sign?"

Uncle Robbie looked at me with a smile and held out his hand.

"Welcome to Winslow Wines, Fiona."

Placing my hand in his, I gave an unsure smile. I had a feeling my life was about to change drastically.

"I cannot believe you're taking over your father's company!" Lydia exclaimed.

Rolling my eyes, I spoke, "Me either."

"Well, at least you're staying in Cali and not moving across the country." She smiled.

"True. Even though I was kind of looking forward to the change."

"Thanks for dinner." She got up from the booth and kissed my cheek. "I have to go get ready to meet Paul."

"Are you nervous?"

"Hell yes, I'm nervous. I hate blind dates."

"Then why did you agree to go out with him?"

"Because I'm desperate to find a man." She pouted. "Spare me your lecture." She put her hand up.

I laughed. "Call me tomorrow and let me know how it went."

"I will. Talk to you soon."

As I was finishing my drink, I gasped when a man slid into the seat across from me. Not just any ordinary man. The man with the dreamy eyes from the casino.

"Well, hello there." He smiled. "Remember me?"

The corners of my mouth curved upwards as I pursed my lips.

"No."

He narrowed his left eye at me and cocked his head. "You're lying. Why not just admit that you remember me?"

"Wait a minute. You're that guy who took my seat at the casino and refused to get up."

"And you're that girl who told me no and then proceeded to beat the hell out of someone's beautiful car in the parking garage." He smirked.

Damn, he was sexy. Wow. I looked down because I swore I was dripping out of my panties. Black designer tailored suit. Expensive, may I add. Hair perfectly styled. Five o'clock shadow that I loved on men so much. But he was full of himself and cocky as shit. Two things I hated most.

"So why did you do it?" he asked as he took the glass from my hand and took a sip of my drink.

"Excuse me. Get your own drink." I took my glass back from him and he grinned.

"All I wanted was a taste so I'd know what you were drinking. Vodka on the rocks. Interesting. Again, why did you do it?"

"He was cheating on me." I smiled.

"Why on earth would anyone cheat on someone as beautiful as you?"

Don't. Don't. Don't fall for it. He's a player.

"Apparently, he's into redheads." I arched my brow.

"What a shame and what a fool."

"Are you here alone?" I asked.

"No. I'm with that woman over there." He pointed to a few tables over. "We just were seated and I glanced over and saw you sitting here alone. I thought I'd stop over and say hi since we already knew each other." His grin widened.

Nice. Another typical asshole.

"We don't know each other. We exchanged a few words and that was it."

"What's your name?" he asked.

"Lucy Collins." I smiled. That was my go-to name when I didn't feel comfortable giving a guy my real name if I suspected he was a creeper or just an asshole.

"Well, it was nice to meet you, Lucy." He got up from the booth.

"Excuse me. Aren't you going to tell me your name?"

"No." He smiled as he walked away.

I watched him as he took a seat at his table. *Jerk.* Sighing, I threw down some cash and headed home. Tomorrow was my first day at Winslow Wines and I needed to make sure I was well rested.

Nathan

Sitting at my desk, I yelled for my assistant, Kylie, to come into my office.

"Yes, Nathan?"

"I want you to find out everything you can about a woman named Lucy Collins. I want an address, phone number, place of employment, etc."

"I'll get right on it."

I was up all night thinking about her. Our small conversation and the way her smile made my cock twitch. Her long blonde hair and the baby blue eyes that twinkled when she looked at me. She remembered me the minute I sat down, yet she played it off as if she didn't. She was feisty. Someone I was up for taming. One night with that beautiful woman and I'd have her in the palm of my hand.

"Hey, Nathan," my right hand and best friend, Will, spoke as he stepped into my office.

"What's up?"

"Christopher Winslow passed away a few days ago and word is that his company is in real trouble."

"Trouble how?"

"In debt up the ass, problems with the vineyards, low inventory and, from what I hear, vendors are threatening to cancel their accounts."

"Hmm. Who's taking over the company? Or are they closing their doors?" I leaned back in my chair.

"I don't know. But what I do know is that a takeover is probably the best thing." He smirked.

"Do some more research. Get the numbers and we'll meet. I've always wanted to dabble in the wine business."

"On it." He began to walk out. "By the way, I ran into Lindsey last night. She told me to tell you that you are a no good, lousy piece of shit cocksucker and she hates you."

I shrugged. "What else is new?"

Just as he walked out, Kylie walked in.

"Here's what I could find on Lucy Collins." She handed me a printout.

"This birthdate puts her at forty-five years old. She isn't forty-five and it says here she's married. She's not married."

"Sorry, Nathan. That's the only Lucy Collins living in Los Angeles."

I sighed. "Thank you."

A smile crossed my face as I sat there shaking my head. She lied to me about her name. Fuck, she just became a whole lot hotter.

CHAPTER 7

Fiona

I took a seat in the chair behind the desk that my father had sat at for almost twenty-five years. Flashbacks of my childhood began to surface when I would come with him to the office sometimes after school or on Saturday afternoons.

"Are you all settled?" Uncle Robbie walked in, pulling me back from the past.

"Yeah." I smiled. "I think I am. I was just remembering all the times I would come here as a kid."

"Doesn't seem all that long ago. Listen, Fiona, did your father ever talk to you about what's going on with the company?"

"No." I frowned. "Why would he?"

"He didn't mention some of the problems to you?"

"Problems? What kind of problems?" I cocked my head.

"The company is in a bit of trouble."

"Okay. Care to explain to me what kind of trouble?"

He sighed. "Your father has made some pretty bad business deals over the past couple of years. With the drought problem, we were having issues with the vineyard that supplies us with the grapes. Their costs went up, the quality went down, and your father didn't like it.

So, he made a couple of deals with some colleagues in the Asian market and it went bad. So bad that it cost the company millions of dollars. We are in the midst of financial ruin, Fiona."

"Why the hell didn't you tell me this before I took over?" I spoke in anger.

"Because this is your father's company. The same company he built from a small loan from the bank all those years ago. He was trying to find new ways to save it."

"Does Rachel know anything about this?"

"No. Your father never told her a thing. He didn't want her to worry."

"Yet he appoints me president and doesn't give a damn if I worry?"

"He and I talked about it and he wanted the company to go to you. His only child. He was fighting like hell to keep the doors open. Winslow Wines was his dream. You of all people should know that."

"I do know that!" I pointed at him. "It's all he ever talked about. The nights he never came home because of some crisis. The vacations that were cancelled because he just couldn't leave the business for a few days. The times he wasn't there for my school functions, my dance recitals, my prom, because he was here. The time he got into a fender bender and my family's life changed forever."

"Your parents' marriage was over way before he met Rachel."

"Get me the reports and the files."

"Sure thing." He got up from his chair. "You're a smart woman, Fiona, and this company needs you. You also need to remember that your father didn't plan on dying and leaving you with this mess."

"Just get me the files, Uncle Robbie." I sighed.

Day one of my new position and already it was a clusterfuck. I couldn't believe this. Picking up my phone, I dialed Lydia.

"What's up, Fi?"

"Drinks tonight. Badly needed drinks."

"Tough first day?"

"You have no idea."

"Drinks it is, then. Pegu club around seven?"

"I'll see you there."

Halfway through the reports, I threw down my pen and rubbed my temples. Uncle Robbie wasn't kidding. The company was in deep shit trouble. Stuffing the rest of the files in my bag, I hopped into my red convertible BMW, drove to Pegu, and slid into the chair across from Lydia. She cocked her head and narrowed her eye.

"You look exhausted. Was it that bad?"

Signaling for the waitress, I ordered an Earl Grey martini.

"Bad isn't a strong enough word. Winslow Wines is in deep financial trouble."

"Wow. How deep?"

"Ocean deep."

"Shit. And your father knew?" She sipped her drink.

"One Earl Grey martini." The waitress set the glass down in front of me. "Would you like to order something?"

"Yes. We'll have the scallops, coconut shrimp, and an order of the chicken wontons."

"Coming right up." She smiled.

"Wow." Lydia laughed. "Really?"

"What? I'm stressed, and I eat when I'm stressed. I'm going to the restroom. I'll be right back."

After freshening up and making my way back to the table, I stopped. Dark gray designer suit, brown hair, perfect profile. Shit. It was him again and he was sitting in my chair.

"Excuse me, but that's my seat." I cocked my head as I stood there with my hands on my hips.

"Well, hello there, Lucy Collins." He smiled as his dreamy green eyes locked on mine.

"What are you doing here?"

"I'm having drinks with my friend over there." He pointed. "I happened to look over and I saw you and your lovely friend sitting down. I was on my way over to say hello when you got up to use the restroom. So, hello."

"Hello." I swallowed hard. "Now that we've got that out of the way, would you kindly remove yourself from my seat? And it looks like your friend over there is waiting for you to return."

He stood up but didn't move out of the way so I could sit down.

"He's fine. He understands that talking to a beautiful woman may take some time."

I gulped.

"I have a question for you."

"You can ask me anything." He smirked.

"Are you stalking me? Because this is the third time we've run into each other."

He chuckled. "No. I'm not stalking you. It's pure coincidence that we keep running into each other. Strange. Wouldn't you say?"

"Very. Now if you'll excuse me, I would like to sit down."

"I'll move in a second after you give me your phone number so I can call you and ask you out to dinner, Lucy." The corners of his mouth curved upwards.

"You mean so you can call me and then sleep with me."

He shrugged. "I didn't say anything about sex, but if that's what you would like, I am more than willing to oblige. I never turn down sex with a beautiful woman."

"I'm sure you don't."

I stood there, assessing him. Studying him. Thinking of my next play.

"I'm sorry," I pouted. "I lied to you. My name isn't Lucy Collins."

"Why would you lie about your name?" He cocked his head.

"Because a woman can never be too careful in this city. But since this is the third time we've run into each other and I can see that you're truly a gentleman, there's no need to lie anymore." I held out my hand. "My name is Elle Hemsworth."

"It's a pleasure to meet you, Elle." He smiled as he placed his hand in mine.

When our fingers touched, I pulled back because something overtook me. A shock, a bolt, a jolt; fuck if I knew. All I knew was that his hand in mine was too much for my body to take. He was breathtakingly gorgeous but a total player. A womanizer. A user.

"Phone number?" he asked.

I gulped as I looked over at Lydia, who was holding a pen in her hand. Taking it from her, I jotted a number down on a white napkin.

"Here. Call me." I folded the napkin in half and handed it to him.

"Oh, I will definitely be calling you." He winked as he began to walk away.

"Wait," I spoke and he turned around. "Your name?"

The corners of his mouth curved into a sly smile. "You'll get my name when I call you."

As he walked away and took his seat with his friend, I sat down and finished off my Earl Grey martini like it was water.

"Hemsworth? Really?" Lydia smirked.

"I had Chris on the brain."

"He's fucking hot as hell. I don't understand why you won't go out with him."

"Because he's a corporate ass. That much I can tell. I just got out of a bad relationship and I'm not about to hop into another one with a guy like him."

"You don't even know him. And who said anything about a relationship? The guy wants to take you to dinner."

"And dinner leads to sex and sex leads to more sex and before you know it, a relationship is formed, and then he'll cheat on me, being the womanizer he is. No thanks." I smiled.

Lydia sat there shaking her head at me. "You have some serious issues."

"You're right." I pointed at her. "I do and I have a failing company to get back on its feet. That's the only thing I'm focusing on. I don't need some sexy corporate ass distracting me. Now let's get the hell out of here before he calls and finds out that I gave him a fake number."

CHAPTER 8

Nathan

"And who was that beautiful creature?" Will smirked as I sat down across from him.

"A woman that I've run into three times now. A woman who gave me a fake name the last time I saw her."

He laughed. "Classic. Did you get her real name this time?"

"I did and her phone number too."

"You sure this time?" He chuckled while leaning back in his chair.

"Let's find out." I pulled my phone from my pocket and dialed the number that was written on the napkin.

"Hello," a rough voice answered.

"I'm calling for Elle Hemsworth."

"Who?"

"Elle Hemsworth."

"Sorry, but you must have the wrong number. I don't know an Elle Hemsworth."

"Thank you." I glared at Will as I hung up. "That bitch."

Will couldn't stop laughing and it was pissing me off.

"Give up, Nathan. She clearly isn't interested in you and she sure as hell knows what she's doing."

"Let's go." I got up from my seat and walked out of the bar.

When I got home, I walked into the living room and poured myself a scotch. Taking it out on the patio, I took a seat in the lounge chair facing the ocean. It was a calm, quiet evening except for the clusterfuck of things running through my head. She wore a navy blue tailored pantsuit and designer heels. Her blonde wavy hair hovered over her shoulders like a goddess's. Her baby blue eyes were made up lightly with just the right amount of shadow and black eyeliner. Gorgeous. Cock raising. Stunning. She was smart. Smart as a whip. The car, the fake name, and a fake number. She wasn't one to be toyed with and she was making that very clear to me. She was strong on the outside, but on the inside, she was broken. Frail. Fragile. Hurt. I couldn't get her out of my mind. Not that night at the casino, not that night at the restaurant, and certainly not tonight at the bar. One taste of her and I would be satisfied. I loved challenges. I thrived on them. Now the problem was finding her again. I wasn't worried. We had run into each three times already and another time was inevitable. Maybe her name, Elle Hemsworth, was real this time, but she didn't trust me enough to give me her real number. Her ex cheated on her. She had trust issues. That douchebag ruined it for me.

The next morning, as I walked into my office, my assistant, Kylie, followed behind.

"Get me everything you can on a woman named Elle Hemsworth."

"Sure thing, Nathan. Los Angeles, I presume?"

"Yes, and do it now."

"I'm on it, sir."

As I took a sip of my coffee and was reviewing the stock market, Will walked in.

"Did you have a chance to look over the information on Winslow Wines last night?" he asked.

"Yes, and they're in serious trouble. Looks like a win for us."

"I found out from one of my contacts that Christopher Winslow appointed his daughter, Fiona Winslow, as president of the company in his will. Apparently, she was to go work for the company after graduating college, but they had some sort of falling out and she ended up going to work for Steiner and Richards Marketing Firm, where she was a huge success but then quit because she was passed up for a promotion."

"Interesting." I narrowed my eye.

"She was then hired by Toth and Sons Marketing Inc. in New York but never made it there because Christopher passed away and left her the family business."

"She should have gone to New York." I smirked.

"I agree. Anyway, we have a meeting this afternoon with her."

"How did you manage that?" I arched my brow.

"I spoke with the financial manager, Robbie Peyton, who is her uncle, and told him that we were interested in helping Winslow Wines get back on its feet. He was open to a meeting and said he'd let Fiona know."

"Excellent. If there's one thing I'm superior at, it's sweeping a woman off her feet. Persuading her to let us into the company won't be hard. Is she married?"

"No."

"Is she hot?"

"I have no clue."

"How old is she?"

"My contact said she's twenty-eight."

"Even better." I smiled. "This, my friend, will be a piece of cake, and we'll be in the wine business before you know it. She's young and I'm sure she knows nothing about running a company. She'll be vulnerable and eager for some help."

"That's exactly what I was thinking. Our meeting is at two o'clock."

"Good job, Will."

"By the way, that woman from last night, Elle."

"What about her?"

"Is that her real name?"

"I don't know yet. I have Kylie checking her out now."

"I can guarantee it isn't and, once again, you've been played." He smirked as he left my office.

Will and I had been friends since the day we met in our freshman year at Berkshire Academy. We both excelled and went on to Harvard, where we graduated with our MBAs and in the top ten percent of our class. He got a job on Wall Street and I followed in my father's footsteps. After the CEO of the company Will worked for was indicted on insider trading charges, the company closed its doors and Will came to work for me at Carter Management Group Inc.

"Excuse me, Nathan," Kylie spoke as she poked her head in the door.

"Come on in. What did you find?"

"I'm sorry. There isn't an Elle Hemsworth in Los Angeles. The only person I could find with that name lives in Anchorage, Alaska."

Slowly closing my eyes, I sighed. "Thank you."

Another fake name to go with the fake phone number. This woman, whoever she was, was now on my nerves. Just wait until the next time I run into her.

CHAPTER 9

*F*iona

A migraine was kicking in as I closed the last file I didn't get to last night. As I rubbed my temples to try and release the tension that was built up in my head, Uncle Robbie walked into my office.

"I need to talk to you about something."

"What about?" I continued to rub my temples. "Wait. Don't answer that question yet. We're seriously fucked here, Uncle Robbie. I honestly don't think we can turn this company around in time."

He took in a deep breath. "I may have a solution to our problem."

"Then by all means, do tell." I waved my hand.

"We have a meeting at two o'clock today with Nathan Carter of the Carter Management Group. He's a venture capitalist and a consultant for struggling companies. His associate, Will Berg, called today and said they may be able to help us."

"Help us how?" I placed my hand on my forehead and leaned back in my chair.

"He has money and a lot of it. He could be a potential investor. A silent partner, so to speak. With his backing, we could have this company back on its feet in no time."

"Is this what my father would have done?"

"I believe he would have."

"And how do we know that he's not going to screw us over like the others did to my father?"

"He's a very reputable man. If there's anyone I would trust, it would be him. His name speaks for itself, just like his father's did."

"Did?"

"He passed away a couple of years ago and Nathan was groomed to take over. I'm surprised you never heard of him."

"Name sounds familiar." I opened my desk drawer and shook a couple of Motrin into my hand.

"Well, they'll be here soon. So be prepared. Just let me do the majority of the talking."

"Why?" I popped the pills into my mouth and chased them down with water. "Don't you trust me?"

"Of course I do, but it's only your second day. You're not really familiar with everything yet."

"Oh, I'm familiar." I got up from my chair and walked into the bathroom. "I'm familiar with how this company is sinking faster than the *Titanic*."

"Just relax, Fiona. I'll show them in as soon as they arrive."

As I took a seat back at my desk, my phone rang. It was Lydia.

"Hello."

"Paul won't return my calls," she spoke in a sad voice.

"The blind date guy?"

"Yes. I can't believe I slept with him and now he won't call me back. Was I that bad?"

"It's not you, honey. It's him. He's a typical male, lousy, woman-using douchebag. Forget about him and move on. You're too good for him."

"You're right. Why is it so hard to find a good man?"

"Because there aren't any good men left in this world." I looked up and froze when I saw who was standing in the doorway of my office. "I—I have to go. I'll call you later."

He stood there, dreamy green eyes, staring at me with his hands tucked neatly in his pants pockets. All six foot of him. *Shit. Shit. Shit.*

"Why I'll be damned," he spoke in a low voice. "Hello, Lucy, or should I say Elle?" His brow raised.

"Hey. Isn't that the chick from last night that gave you the bogus phone number?" his friend asked.

"You two know each other?" Uncle Robbie asked.

"Not really. Could the two of you give us a moment before we start our meeting?" Nathan asked.

"Fiona?" Uncle Robbie looked at me.

"It's fine." I sighed.

After Uncle Robbie and the other guy walked out, the man, who I presumed was Nathan Carter, stood in the doorway, glaring at me.

"Well, are you just going to stand there? Come in and sit down. Obviously, you have a few things you want to say to me before our meeting."

"Oh, I have a lot to say, Lucy, Elle, or whatever the hell your name is."

"Fiona Winslow." I cocked my head.

"Two fake names and a fake number. Why?"

"Because I'm not interested. Okay? There, I said it."

"All right, then. That's all you had to say in the first place. Let's start over. Hello, Fiona Winslow, I'm Nathan Carter." He held out his hand and I was afraid to touch it.

Hesitantly placing my hand in his and feeling the same spark that was there last night, I spoke, "It's nice to meet you, Nathan."

"Now that I got your real name squared away, shall we start our meeting?"

"Yes." I smiled.

After calling in Uncle Robbie and Will, we took a seat at the round table that sat inside my office. The same table that I used to sit at and color pictures when I was a kid.

Nathan

Fiona Winslow. Beautiful name, beautiful woman, and the president of Winslow Wines. She was smart. Tough. Actually, she was brilliant for the little stunt she pulled on me. Taking over her company was going to be tougher than I thought. Of all the women in Los Angeles to be attracted to, why did it have to be her?

"So how can you help us, Nathan?" she asked.

"From what I hear, you're low on funds. Your inventory is low and vendors have already begun pulling out of their contracts. Now, I can help you with the funds and we can turn this company around."

"Why the interest in Winslow Wines?" She narrowed her eye.

Leaning back in my chair, I spoke, "I've always wanted to dabble in the wine business. You make wine, you're struggling, I can help, so it's a win-win for all of us. I will need to see all your financial reports first."

"Of course. Don't venture capitalists usually take on start-up companies?"

"Usually. But I like to take risks." I smirked. "And I believe Winslow Wines can be turned around and make even more money than before. I give advice on how you can do that, Fiona. That's my job. We'd work together to restructure the company to maximize its profits. We'd take a look at what went wrong and how to fix it. Everything is fixable." I winked.

"I'll think about it." She got up from her seat. "Uncle Robbie, get them the financial reports. Put together a proposal and get back with me," she spoke.

"Will, go with Robbie and get the reports. I'll wait here for you," I spoke as I stared at Fiona.

As the two of them left the office, I got up from my seat and walked over to where she was leaning up against her desk.

"I think you'll like my proposal. I'll need your phone number to contact you when it's ready and we can meet."

"You have my office phone number."

"Not good enough. What if I have a question about something I see in the reports and it's after business hours? I will need to be able to get hold of you at all hours."

"Fine." She reached over, grabbed a piece of paper and a pen, and jotted down her number.

"Thank you." I took the paper from her hand and our fingers lightly brushed against each other's.

"I got the reports, Nathan. We should get going," Will spoke.

"I'll be in touch, Miss Winslow."

With a small smile, she gave me a nod. As I was walking out of her office, I stopped and pulled my phone from my pocket, dialing the number that was written down on the paper. Suddenly, the cell phone sitting on her desk began to ring.

"Just checking." I smiled at her.

Walking out of the building, Will placed his hand on my shoulder.

"All I can say, Nathan, is that you have your work cut out for you with Miss Fiona Winslow. Damn, I couldn't believe my eyes when I saw her sitting behind that desk."

"I'm not worried about it. I can handle her. Never underestimate me, my friend." I slid into the back of the car.

"I'm not, but I'm also not underestimating her. Fuck. Sexy and brains. Rare combo these days. The women we date are sexy, but as for the brains, not so much." He chuckled.

"Leave her to me. Not only will she be in my bed, but she'll also be signing over her company to me." I stared out the passenger window.

CHAPTER 10

*F*iona

"No. No. No." I banged my forehead against the desk.

"What on earth are you doing?" Uncle Robbie asked as he walked in. "And thank you for taking over the meeting."

"That man! I'm not sure we can do business with him." I rubbed my forehead.

"Why not? And who? Nathan Carter?"

"Yes. I don't trust him." I got up from my chair and walked to the front of my desk. "He's sneaky and he's a game player." I scrunched up my hands in front of my face. "He's—He's—a man! A womanizer, and he doesn't take no for an answer."

"What are you talking about, Fiona?"

Leaning back on my desk, I spoke, "I met him or, should I say, ran into him a couple of times, the most recent being last night. The first time we saw each other was at the casino when he refused to get up from the stool at the bar I was sitting at when I went to the restroom. The second time, I was alone in a restaurant and he slid in the seat across from me, took a sip of my drink, and demanded to know my name. So I lied and told him my name was Lucy. Then last night, we ran into each other at Pegu when I came back from the bathroom, and he was sitting in my seat across from Lydia. We exchanged a few words and then I told him I lied about my name. I told him my real name was Elle and I gave him a fake phone number. Now he just so happens to be the man that could save this company."

"Shit, Fiona. Why would you do that?"

"Because I didn't trust him." I threw my hands in the air. "This is karma, Uncle Robbie. Karma for what I did to John."

"And what exactly did you do to John?" He frowned.

"Umm. I broke up with him over text messages." I quietly sank back into my chair and cupped my face in my hands.

"Listen, sweetheart. You're just having a moment right now. So much has happened over the past few days and you're still trying to process it. Look, go home. Take a hot bath. Relax. Read a book and have a glass of wine. Forget about Nathan and work for tonight. It's all going to work out."

"You're right. I need to relax." I grabbed my purse from the drawer.

Walking over to Uncle Robbie, I laid my head on his shoulder.

"I don't know if I can do this."

"You can and you will. Where's that little girl that used to come in here and pretend she owned the place? Ordering me around, asking me for reports, telling me what we should do? Do you remember her?"

A smile crossed my lips. "Yeah. I remember her."

"That's my darling niece. Your mother would be so proud of you. Now get out of here and go home. I'll see you tomorrow."

Walking through the front door, I kicked off my heels and headed straight to the kitchen for a glass of wine. Taking my glass upstairs, I went into the bathroom and started the water, adding a few drops of lavender oil and a capful of lavender bubble bath. Relaxation was going to be my friend tonight. As I laid back against my bath pillow with a warm cloth over my eyes, I inhaled the lavender scent that filled my senses. A calming sensation flowed throughout my body. I was finally relaxed, taking in the glory of the peace and finally getting my mind to rest, until my doorbell rang. My eyes flew open and I sat there for a moment, letting whoever it was believe no one was home.

Another ring. Suddenly, my phone beeped with a text message from a number I didn't recognize.

"It's Nathan and I'm standing at your front door. I'm letting you know in case you're afraid it's a stranger and refuse to answer it. Which, by the way, you shouldn't answer it unless you know who it is. So, I'm letting you know it's me. Not a stranger."

Are you kidding me? How the hell did he know where I lived? Climbing out the tub, I dried off as quickly as I could and threw on the closest thing to me, which was my short navy blue satin robe. The nerve of him just showing up at my place unannounced. I stormed down the stairs, unlocked the door, and flung it open. His eyes raked over me from head to toe and then from toe to head as the corners of his mouth curved up into a smile.

"Am I interrupting something?"

"Yes. As a matter of fact, you interrupted my nice, peaceful hot bath. What are you doing here, Nathan?" I placed my hand on my hip. "Or better yet. How the hell did you know where I lived?"

"You aren't that hard to find, sweetheart." He smirked. "May I come in?"

"Why not?" I motioned for him to come inside. "Just give me a minute so I can change."

"Why change? I happen to like what you're wearing now. I think you should leave it on." He winked.

"And I don't care what you think. I'll be right back. Go sit down in the living room or something."

"Are you always this rude to your houseguests?" he shouted as I walked up the stairs.

"Only when they stop by unannounced!" I shouted back.

"I sent you a text that I was here, so it wasn't unannounced."

I stopped at the top of the stairs, turned my head, and looked at him.

"You were already standing at my front door before you sent me the text. Therefore, you showed up unannounced."

He chuckled and I changed into a pair of yoga pants and a tank top.

"So why are you here, Nathan?" I asked as I walked into the living room.

"I would like us to have dinner together tonight."

"Why?"

"Why not?" He smirked.

"You've been trying to get me to go out with you since the first time I saw you at the casino. Aha!" I pointed at him.

"What?" He arched his brow.

"That's why you want to help Winslow Wines out. You're using that as a way to get me to go out with you. Oh, you're good." I stood there, shaking my finger at him.

"Fiona. I had no idea you were the woman who's the president of Winslow Wines. If you recall, you gave me two fake names. I had no clue who you really were. I was just as shocked as you were when I walked into your office. Listen, on a serious note, I need to get to know the people who are running the company that I want to invest in. It's all business. Nothing personal, I promise. What if you were some kind of crazy lunatic person who goes around smashing up pretty little expensive cars? Oh wait. You are." He snickered.

"Can you please just forget that you saw me do that? It wasn't one of my finer moments."

"So you didn't enjoy it?"

"Okay. Maybe just a little." I grinned. "So now you know that I'm a crazy lunatic person. Isn't that enough?"

He tucked his hands into his pockets as a small smile escaped his lips. "I like crazy. So how about that business dinner? Nothing big. We'll just grab something to eat, talk, and then call it a night. I know you have to be at the office early as well as I."

Did I trust him? He was dangerous. That much I knew. And not in a creepy, deranged, murderous type of way. He was dangerously good looking. Handsome. Sexy. A danger to me because I couldn't help but to think what it would be like to have him on top and inside of me. And also a danger because every time I found myself in his presence, an incredible ache between my legs formed without hesitation.

"It's only four thirty. You want to go now?"

"Yes. That is, if you can hurry up and get ready."

"Can you give me fifteen?"

"Fifteen minutes is fine." He smiled.

I headed to my bedroom and pulled out a red spaghetti strap sundress from the closet. Stepping in front of the bathroom mirror, I quickly touched up my makeup before pulling out the clip that held my hair up. I ran a brush through it and lightly sprayed the ends and then I slipped my feet into a low heel red strappy sandal and headed back downstairs.

"Okay. I'm ready."

Nathan turned around and whistled. "You look great. Shall we go?"

"Yes." I smiled as I walked out the front door and slid into the back of his limo.

"Jason, I would like you to meet Fiona Winslow. Fiona, this is my driver, Jason."

"Nice to meet you, Fiona." He grinned.

"Nice to meet you too, Jason."

As the limo pulled away, I was curious as to where Nathan was taking me to dinner.

"Was there a certain restaurant you had in mind?" I asked.

"I hope you like Italian food."

"I do."

"Good. There's this great little restaurant that serves the best Italian cuisine I'd ever had in my life."

"What's it called?"

"Acquerello."

"Nice name. Where's it located? I don't think I've ever heard of it."

The corners of his mouth curved upwards. "San Francisco."

"Excuse me? We're having dinner in San Francisco?"

"Yes. We're taking my private jet. We'll be there in no time."

"You're kidding, right?" I narrowed my eye at him.

"I don't kid about Italian perfection."

I sat there, dazed and confused. I couldn't believe our business dinner was going to be in San Francisco.

"Who does that?" I looked at him.

"Who does what?"

"Flies off to San Francisco for dinner?"

"A lot of people. It's not a big deal."

"But it is because the flight time from Los Angeles to San Francisco is about an hour and a half."

"Actually, I can get us there in an hour and ten. To drive is about six hours on a good traffic day. So flying to San Francisco is faster." He grinned.

I gave up. Arguing with him was exhausting me already. San Francisco was beautiful and I guess having dinner there wouldn't be so bad.

CHAPTER 11

Nathan

I could tell she was nervous about having dinner in San Francisco, but damn, did she look beautiful. I was actually a little surprised she didn't throw me out of her condo. Seeing her in that silk robe with her hard nipples poking through sent my cock into a spastic fit. God, what I wouldn't give to have a taste of her sweet lips, and not just the ones attached to her face. She was one woman I couldn't stop thinking of since the first night I saw her. She occupied a space in my mind. I'd never thought about a woman like this before. So why her? What was it about Fiona Winslow that had me so curious about her? Maybe it was the fact that she was a challenge. After all, she did tell me no. But now, the stakes were raised because I was after her company, which made her even more beautiful and delicious.

We arrived at Acquerello and were promptly seated at my usual table tucked away in a quiet corner.

"Welcome back, Mr. Carter," the pretty brunette spoke as she handed us our menus.

"Thank you."

"Do you dine here often?" Fiona asked as she opened her menu.

"Enough." I smirked.

"Hello, Mr. Carter," our waitress named Carly spoke.

"Hello, Carly. How are you?"

"I'm doing good. Thanks for asking. What can I start you off with to drink?"

"I'll have—" Fiona started to speak.

"We'll have a bottle of Bibi Graetz, Ansonica Toscana Bugia."

"Excellent." She smiled as she walked away.

"What did you just order?" she asked as she narrowed her eye at me.

"You'll see."

"So like, do you know everyone here?" she asked. "If not, they sure seem to know who you are."

"I know a lot of people all over the world." I smirked.

"I'm sure you do." She arched her brow. "And I'm sure a majority of them are women."

Carly walked over to the table with the bottle and two glasses. After pouring some in one glass, she handed it to me for my approval.

"Hand the glass to Miss Winslow. She can taste this one."

Fiona looked at me, took the glass from Carly, swirled it around, sniffed it, and then took a sip. A smile graced her face.

"It's perfect," she spoke to Carly.

After placing our order, Fiona glared at me for a moment.

"That's some damn good wine."

"I knew you'd like it. Now, enough about the wine. Tell me about yourself."

"Tell me about yourself first." She smirked as she sipped from her glass.

"I do believe I asked first." I cocked my head.

"Then I'll give you the basics because that's all you need to know. I was born and raised in Anaheim. Graduated from UCLA with my MBA. Started working for Steiner & Richards Marketing firm as soon as I graduated and now I'm running my father's company."

"Is there a reason you didn't work at Winslow Wines when you graduated college?" I asked.

She looked down as she placed her napkin on her lap.

"There was a period of time when my father and I didn't really speak. It was best that I did my own thing."

"He must have been hurt that his daughter wouldn't work for the family business," I spoke as I picked up my glass.

"Yeah, well, he hurt me."

❧

Fiona

I wasn't comfortable talking to Nathan about my family and I needed to change the subject quickly.

"This restaurant is beautiful."

It was elegant with the burnt orange walls and dark cherry moldings. A mixture of tables filled the place. Some round, some square, and some rectangular. All draped with white linen tablecloths, matching napkins, and fine china. The setting was cozy, with low lighting that gave way to an intimate atmosphere. Candles burning in crystal hurricanes gave off a soft glow and subtle Italian music filled the air.

"Thank you. So how did your father hurt you?"

I gave him a perplexed look.

"Why did you say thank you? Do you own the place or something?"

"In fact, I do." He smiled.

"Yeah, right." I laughed as I took a sip of my wine.

"I do. There were a lot of things wrong when they first opened and business was pretty bad. They were on the verge of closing up only after a year until I saw the potential this place had. I became a partner, did some remodeling, hired the best chefs I could find, restructured the business, and the end result," he held out his hands, "this. And reservations book up months at a time."

"Impressive." My lips gave way to a small smile.

"See, not all businesses that are in trouble have to close their doors. And I believe that Winslow Wines can be saved. Now, back to how your father hurt you."

I narrowed my eyes at him for a moment.

"Why are you so interested in how my father hurt me?"

"I would like to know the things that hurt my potential business partners so I can make sure I don't make the same mistakes."

Oh, he was smooth. I wondered if that came naturally or he took some sort of classes.

"My parents divorced when I was eighteen because my father met someone else and left my mother for her."

"I'm sorry to hear that. So cheating is a big issue for you?"

Huh? Wasn't it for anyone?

"Of course. Nobody likes to be cheated on. If a man or woman wants to date someone else or sleep with them, then they need to be honest about it before doing it. It's called having morals," I spoke with seriousness.

"And that right there is the reason I don't get involved in relationships." He smirked. "Much more trouble than what it's worth."

"I'll have to agree with you, Mr. Carter. After this last little mishap with John, I'm seeing things in a different light." I held up my wine glass to him.

"Too many complications and expectations. That's why I don't stick around after sex. I do the dirty deed and walk away, with no shame, may I add." His glass lightly tapped mine.

Damn, I hated his attitude, but fuck if he wasn't making my panties wet.

"I'm curious to know." He smirked. "Does John know you were the one who wrecked his car?"

I let out a soft laugh. "No."

"You went to a lot of trouble to disguise yourself. How did you know where he'd be that night? I'm assuming he didn't tell you where he was going."

"No. He told me that he had to work late, again. I had suspected for some time that he was cheating. So, after I read his text message canceling our date, I hacked into his phone."

A wave of shock overtook his handsome face.

"Excuse me? You hacked into his phone?"

"Yes, and I read the text messages between him and his lover. That's how I knew where he was that night. When his mistress got up to go to the restroom, I followed her. She provided some pretty good information."

"Like? Did she know who you were?"

"She didn't have a clue. They had been dating for six months."

"Ouch. How long were the two of you dating for?"

"A year."

"Double ouch." His brow raised.

"I would have found out sooner, but I was too busy working my ass off for a promotion at the marketing firm I was at. And what a waste of time that was." I rolled my eyes.

"I assume you didn't get it?"

"No, I didn't, and the only reason I didn't get it was because the owner was fucking the woman who got it over me. Did I mention he was married?"

"Oh boy. Well, I'd say it all worked out in your favor because you are now the president of your father's company."

"Failing company." I held up my glass before taking a sip.

CHAPTER 12

Fiona

After finishing a delicious dinner, we headed to Nathan's plane to go home. I still hadn't gotten any information on him or about his life. I needed to know whom I was up against. His intentions of helping Winslow Wines might have been good. Or he led me to believe they were. There was something about that sexy man I didn't trust, and I had a feeling he was playing a game. Call it my woman's intuition, and in every game, there's more than one player. Hence, the second player was me.

As we were sitting on the plane, I glanced over at Nathan, who was on his iPad.

"How did you end up where you are? You can't be any older than I am."

"I'm thirty. My father started the company before I was born, and after graduating college, I stepped in as vice president. When he passed away two years ago, I took over, tripling profits every quarter. I guess you can say that I'm a smarter businessman than my father was." He smirked. "Enough about me. I'm still baffled at the fact that you hacked into your ex's phone. How on earth did you manage that?"

I smiled. "I have a friend who taught me a thing or two. He's actually a genius."

"Should I be worried that you know how to do that?"

"You should always be worried with anything to do with me." I winked.

He chuckled. "I like a woman with confidence."

Nathan continued working on his iPad while I stared out the window. He was the one with all the confidence. You could tell just by the way he walked and carried himself. He turned me on more than any man ever had and having sex with him would probably be the most incredible journey I'd ever gone on. Okay, it would be the only incredible journey I'd ever gone on. I had never been on an incredible journey before. But him, Nathan Carter; I would bet my life that he was a god between the sheets. I tightened my legs at the thought, for the ache that resided down below was growing stronger.

The ride home in the limo didn't consist of much conversation because Nathan was on a business call.

"Sorry about that," he spoke as he placed his phone in his pocket.

"Don't worry about it. You're a very busy man." I smiled.

The limo pulled up in my driveway and Nathan climbed out first, holding out his hand to help me.

"Thank you." I felt myself tremble at the mere touch of my hand in his.

After he walked me to the door, I placed the key in the lock and opened it.

"Thank you for a lovely dinner." I smiled.

"You're welcome. Thank you for not kicking me out for showing up unannounced."

The smile on my lips stayed put. "So you admit you showed up unannounced?"

"Perhaps I should have called before I arrived." He gently placed his hand on the side of my face.

My heart began to pick up its pace, beating rapidly as if it was trying to escape me. I swallowed hard as his eyes stared into mine. I needed to break free from the trance he had me in, but I couldn't move. I was frozen, paralyzed by this sexy man with a look of hunger in his eyes. His head dipped lower until his lips were mere inches from mine. His warm breath swept over me, causing a trembling sensation throughout my body.

"I should get inside. It's late," I whispered in a soft voice.

"Yeah and I should be getting home, but I need to kiss you first."

"I'm not sure that's a good idea. Business and pleasure don't mix."

"Tonight, I'm not a business man. I'm just an ordinary guy who wants to kiss the lips of a beautiful woman."

"Okay," I spoke like the idiot I was.

His lips gently brushed against mine and I returned his kiss. He stopped and stared at me, his hand still cupping my face.

"Once wasn't enough," he spoke as he leaned in and kissed me again.

My panties were already soaked with excitement and my lady parts were on fire, screaming with desire as I imagined him naked and hovering over me. My lips parted as his tongue met mine. His teeth lightly nipped my bottom lip, sending my body into overdrive with pleasure.

"I think maybe we should step inside unless you want to give your neighbors a show," he softly moaned.

I was worried because I wasn't anyone special to him. I was just another woman who he was going to fuck for his own entertainment. But his lips, his tongue, and his touch made me crave more, an indescribable feeling where, suddenly, I didn't care. My body wanted him, all of him, and he wanted me. The game was on and I was more than willing to play along.

"Yes. I think we should go inside." I smiled as I led him into the house.

He gripped my hips from behind as his lips explored my neck. I hadn't felt this good or wanted in a very long time. Removing his hand from my waist, he took the bottom of my dress and slightly pulled it up until his fingers reached the silk fabric of my panties. A low moan rumbled from his chest as he pushed them aside and plunged a finger deep inside me without hesitation. I gasped, not only from his touch, but from the hardness that was pressed against my lower back.

"You feel so good," he moaned. "And I'm going to make you come this way first before I take you upstairs and devour the rest of you."

His fingers moved seductively in and out of me and around in circles, hitting my G spot and sending my body over the edge. My soft moans became louder as an orgasm overtook me.

"Yes. That's what I wanted," he whispered in my ear.

Nathan

Removing my fingers, I turned her around and lightly traced her lips before leaning down for a kiss, tasting the pleasure that came from her. I wanted to take it slow because I wanted to devour every part of her perfect body. Taking my hand, she led me up the stairs and to her bedroom. I stopped her a few feet from the bed and reached around, unzipping her from behind and slowly taking down her straps, letting her dress fall to her feet. Her hourglass figure, her cleavage from the sexy black lace bra she was wearing and matching lace panties, was already making my hard cock drip with excitement. She was perfection if I ever saw it. Unhooking her bra, I then removed it and tossed it on the bed. Her supple breasts—perfect size, natural—and her hard nipples begged for attention. I unbuttoned my shirt as our eyes never left each other's and tossed it on the floor. Her fingers reached for my belt and unbuckled it as my hands roamed up and down her sides and up to her bare breasts, cupping them with delight, feeling the softness of them. I was ready to explode, but I needed to take it slow with her. Softly kissing her lips, I slid my tongue down the front of her neck and across her collarbone, making my way down to her breasts, taking them in my mouth one at a time.

She had successfully unbuttoned my pants and slid them off my hips, stroking my hard cock through the fabric of my underwear. Her touch was sensual and erotic. Turning her around, I laid her face down on the bed and let my tongue roam across the soft skin of her back, tracing little circles around her spine until I reached her perfectly round-shaped ass. Gripping the top of her panties with my teeth, I pulled them down and a sensual moan escaped her. After taking down my underwear, I gripped her hips and rolled her over on her back. Spreading her legs, I buried my head between her thighs, softly kissing and rolling my tongue around her swollen and beautiful pussy that begged for more. Her hands gripped my head as she thrust her hips up in excitement. She was getting ready to come as her hands left my head and tightly gripped the comforter. My fingers roamed while my tongue explored the rest of her. Her breathing became hitched as she shouted "yes" and her body released itself to me.

I wasn't wasting any more time. I needed to be inside her, fucking her and making her scream with pleasure. I took a condom from my pants pocket and ripped it open while staring down at her and seeing the excitement that resided in her eyes. After slipping it on, I grabbed her wrists and brought them over her head, gripping them tight as my cock thrust inside her. My mouth smashed into hers in the heat of the moment as I moved rapidly in and out of her. Her legs wrapped around my waist, forcing me to deepen inside her. She struggled to get out of my grip and was successful in bringing her hands to my face as our lips were locked tightly together. The buildup was coming. Her pussy tightened and a rush of warmth swept over me.

"Fuck, Fiona. I'm going to come already," I panted as I pushed into her one last time and my cock exploded.

Collapsing on top of her, I could feel her heart beating at the same rhythm as mine. Thoughts were filling my head. Things I didn't want to think about. Things I never thought about. Before rolling off, I kissed her.

"You were wonderful," I spoke as I stroked her cheek, got up from the bed, and disposed of the condom in the bathroom.

"So were you." She smiled as she slipped on her robe. "Thanks, Nathan. I'll talk to you soon."

Shit. I hadn't even put on my clothes yet and she was already kicking me out.

"How about one drink before I go?"

She walked into the bathroom and ran a brush through her hair.

"No. It's late and I'm tired, so I think it's best you leave now."

"Okay. If that's what you want." I slipped into my clothes.

"I do." She smiled as she walked out of the bathroom.

She escorted me to the door and, before I left, I ran my hand through her hair. "I'll call you tomorrow when the proposal is ready to be looked at."

"Sounds good. Have a good night."

"You too." I frowned as I kissed her forehead. She was all too eager for me to leave.

When I climbed into the limo, Jason looked at me.

"I like her, Nathan. I hope you didn't hurt her too much by leaving."

"No. Actually, she kicked me out. I wanted to stay for a drink and she told me no."

Jason chuckled. "Oh boy. I knew I liked her for a reason."

"Just drive." I sighed.

CHAPTER 13

Fiona

After shutting the door, I leaned my back against it and slowly slid to the floor. I let out a long sigh as I thought about what just happened. He was more than a god between the sheets. I knew he'd be good, but I didn't think it was possible to be that good. The way he made my body feel was euphoric and something I would never forget. I was lost in him during sex. His hands, his tongue, his lips, and his body. My god, his body. Perfect. Hard. Toned in every possible way. Every muscle defined to perfection. He was strong and I'd never forget how his arms felt around me. He'd taken me places that I'd never been to before. My body and my mind, all to another world. A world without a care or worry. He made me forget who I was, who he was. I could still feel him inside of me. Weird, right? Sex was just sex, but tonight, this wasn't just sex. I couldn't explain it, for I was at a loss for words. I'd never believed in magic before, until now.

I shook my head and brought myself back to reality. I needed to remember whom I was dealing with. He was Nathan Carter and he was a man with an agenda. He wanted to help my company, but at what cost?

The next morning, I walked into the office with my coffee in hand.

Josh, my assistant, followed me in. A few days before my father passed away, his secretary of twenty-five years, Rita, retired to take care of her ailing husband. Josh was a replacement the temp agency sent and when I started, I decided just to hire him full-time. I didn't want the added stress of having to find someone. He was already here, I liked him, and he liked me. At least I thought he did.

"You have a board meeting in thirty minutes."

"Today? Why am I just finding out about this now? And by the way, good morning, Josh."

"Good morning, Fiona. It's on your calendar. Have you not checked it?" he asked with a slight attitude.

"No. I guess I didn't. Do I have to go?" I whined as I sat down in my chair.

"Yes."

"Okay, Josh. Here's how it's going to go. You're my assistant, right?"

"Yes." He narrowed his eye.

"So we're going to be stuck together like glue. Got it? No matter what I ask you to do, even if it's out of the business realm, you are to do it. Me and you," I pointed, "are going to become very close. I don't let too many people into my life, but you, I'm letting you in because I need you. And what I ask you to do stays between us. Got it?"

"Yes. I got it." His brow arched. "If there's nothing else, I have to get back to my desk."

"Okay. Go work away." I smiled.

I needed to prepare myself to get chastised by the board members. I was up all night thinking about Nathan. Good call on my part kicking him out right after sex. He needed to know that I was in control. Sex with him never should have happened, but it did and I was prepared to face the consequences of my actions, whatever they might be. Only time would tell.

My phone started to ring and Lydia was calling.

"Good morning," I answered.

"Morning. Hey, can we meet after work? There's something I need to tell you."

"Sure. I was going to call you later because there's something I need to tell you too."

"Okay. How about your house? I'll stop on the way and grab some Chinese food for us."

"Sounds good. Don't forget the egg rolls and the fortune cookies."

"I won't," she spoke in a low voice.

"Hey, are you okay?" I asked with concern.

"Yeah. I'm okay. I'll see you later."

Something was off with her. But I'd have to wait until later to find out what was going on. Right now, I had a board meeting to focus on.

Nathan

I was up all night thinking about Fiona, and I needed to know exactly whom I was dealing with.

"Thanks for meeting with me, Bryce," I spoke as we shook hands and I took a seat across from his desk.

"Not a problem, Nathan. I will admit that I was surprised to get your call. What can I do for you?" He leaned back in his chair and interlaced his fingers.

"I'm inquiring about one of your ex-employees, Fiona Winslow."

"What about her?"

"What kind of employee was she? And I want the truth. From what I've heard, she was in line for a big promotion."

"She was and, unfortunately, the promotion went to someone else. But she was a damn good employee. Very smart. Probably one of the smartest and most creative people I'd ever had work for me."

"Care to tell me how?"

"Well." He removed his black-rimmed glasses from his face. "She brought on more accounts than anyone else had. One of my other employees screwed up with Nike and they were on the verge of leaving until Fiona stepped in and saved it. She made them promises and followed through with them. Made them happy."

"So why didn't she get the promotion?"

"It's a little complicated. May I ask why you're so interested in her? You do know that she's taken over running her father's company."

"Yes, I know, and that company is in a lot of trouble. I'm thinking about becoming an investor, but I need to know whom I'm dealing with first."

"If anyone can turn that company around, it's Fiona. Not only is she business smart, but she's street smart too. People adore her. She has a way of taking her most brutal enemy and making them her friend. She has a way with people. Like I said, she would have had that promotion without hesitation if—"

"If you were thinking with your head instead of your dick, right?" I smirked.

He looked down in embarrassment. "You know what it's like, Nathan, in our world."

Getting up from my seat, I spoke, "No, actually, I don't, Bryce, because I don't let my dick get in the way of business decisions. Business is business and pleasure is pleasure. You need to keep the two separate or else you'll sink. Thanks again for meeting with me." I walked out of his office.

Fiona

"Who the hell do they think they are?" I scowled as I stormed out of the boardroom.

"The board of directors," Uncle Robbie replied.

"They're giving me six months to turn this company around or they're voting me out. Six months is absurd. I can't do that in six months and they know it! This is their way of trying to force me out."

"Calm down, Fiona." Uncle Robbie clasped my shoulders. "Don't let them get to you."

"How can I not? This is my family's company and I'll be damned if I'm forced out of it."

"There's the fierce woman I've been waiting for." He smiled as he kissed my forehead. "I have another meeting. I'll fill you in later."

Taking a seat behind my desk, I laid my head down.

"Are you okay, Fiona?" Josh asked.

"No." I lifted my head up. "I want everything you can find on each of the board members."

"Huh?"

"I want information on each of the board members. Anything you can dig up and dig deep, really deep. They're corporate thugs and I'm sure they have skeletons in their closet."

"Umm. Okay. Anything else?"

"Not right now."

My phone rang, and when I looked over, I saw it was Nathan. Ugh. Now was not a good time.

"Hello."

"Hello, beautiful. I'm thinking dinner tonight. What do you say?"

"I can't. I'm having dinner with Lydia."

"Can't you have dinner with her another night?"

"No. I already made plans. I'm sure you have plenty of friends that would love to have dinner with you tonight."

"That's not the point. I wanted to have dinner with you to discuss a few things."

"Well, you're going to have to wait. I already have plans."

"Don't you think that business is a little more important?"

"Not in all cases. My best friend needs me and I'm going to be there for her."

"Suit yourself. I might have to reconsider my offer to help your company."

I removed my phone from my ear and looked at it. Was he serious? All because I wouldn't have dinner with him? *Asshole.*

"Do what you have to do then. I have to go." *Click.* "JOSH!" I yelled.

"Yes, Fiona?" He walked into my office.

"Call the vineyard. I'm heading out there for a meeting tomorrow. Wait. No. Don't call them. I'll just make a surprise visit."

"Okay." He sighed as he walked out of my office.

CHAPTER 14

Nathan

"Damn it!" I shouted as I threw my phone across my desk.

"Is everything okay, Nathan?" Kylie asked with concern as she stepped into my office.

"No. Everything is not okay."

"Anything I can do to help?"

"Yes. Get Miss Winslow to have dinner with me tonight."

"I'll call her right now, sir."

I sighed. "Don't bother. She already has plans with her friend. Apparently, her friends are more important than her company, which is the reason why she will fail at turning it around."

"I agree, Nathan." She nodded.

"Is the proposal ready yet?"

"Almost. The legal department is checking it over one last time to make sure everything is in place."

"I need it tonight. Make sure it's on my desk by seven o'clock."

"Yes, sir. Is there anything else?"

"No."

If she wouldn't have dinner with me tonight, then she would have lunch with me tomorrow. Leaning back in my chair, I recalled our phone conversation. She sounded stressed out. There was no way she could bring that company back without me and my help.

"Hey, Nathan. You got a minute?" Will asked as he walked in.

"What's up?"

"My contact said that there was a board meeting at Winslow Wines this afternoon and they gave Fiona six months to turn it around or else she was out."

"Interesting." I cocked my head. "Six months is not a lot of time. It sounds like to me they aren't happy with her taking over."

"They aren't."

"Then all she has to do is sign the contracts and her problems will be solved."

"I'm not too sure she's going to sign them once she sees the terms."

"Then she's cutting her own throat. But don't worry; I'll get her to sign them. Trust me." I smiled.

"I have no doubt you will, but at what price?" His brow arched.

"Don't you worry about that. I'll take care of Miss Winslow."

Fiona

Long-ass day. Pounding headache. Grumbling belly from the lack of food it got today. Sighing, I set down my purse in the hallway before heading into the kitchen, only to find Lydia standing over the island, gripping the edge of the black-specked marble countertop.

"Hey. Are you okay?"

She looked up at me with a small smile. "I'm okay. Just tired. Long day."

"I hear you. My day sucked too," I spoke as I grabbed two plates from the upper cabinet and handed them to her.

As I stared at her, I knew something wasn't right. But I wasn't going to force the issue until she was ready to tell me. She took the plates over to the table and I grabbed two wine glasses and a bottle of wine.

"Oh. None for me." She held up her hand.

"What? Why? Are you pregnant or something?" I laughed as I filled both glasses.

"Yeah. I am," she spoke in a low voice.

"What?" I set the wine bottle on the counter and stared at her in disbelief.

Tears began to fill her eyes as she pursed her lips together and nodded her head.

"Aw, sweetie." I walked over and wrapped my arms around her, which sent her into a total crying mess.

"I just found out last night. I wanted to call you, but I knew you were with Nathan. I took four pregnancy tests and they all came back positive. Every single one of them." She sniffled.

"Who's the father?" I broke our embrace.

"Jeremy."

"Which one was he?" I asked with a twisted face.

"The one I met on Tinder. You remember. The one who said he lived in L.A. but really he was only here on business for the weekend and then he gave me a fake phone number and deleted his profile."

"Oh yeah. Are you sure it's him? I mean, you've had a lot of one-night stands."

"He was the only one I didn't use a condom with."

"But you're on birth control," I spoke as I took the cartons of food over to the table.

"I was in between birth control when I was with him."

"Whatever decision you make; I'll stand by you."

"I'm going to keep it. I have a job, make good money, have a nice home, and there's no reason I shouldn't. There are a lot of women who are single moms. Look at Jessica from finance. She used a sperm donor. And I'm not getting any younger."

"You're only twenty-eight." I smiled as I bit into my egg roll.

"Exactly, and with all the douchebags out there, I may never find someone. This could be my only chance to have a kid."

"Then I'm happy for you. Oh my God, we're having a baby." I smiled as I grabbed hold of her hand and squeezed it tight.

After Lydia left, I finished cleaning up the kitchen and headed upstairs. After changing into my pajamas, I climbed into bed. Just as I snuggled in for the night, after a day of longing for my fluffy pillow, my phone beeped. Rolling over, I picked it up from the nightstand and saw a text message from Nathan. Why was he texting me so late?

"I just wanted to say that I was extremely disappointed that you said no to having dinner with me tonight."

"My friend needed me."

"Maybe I needed you."

A small smile crossed my lips as I read his message.

"I highly doubt that, Mr. Carter."

"Believe what you will. We'll talk tomorrow. Good night."

"Good night."

Setting my phone on the nightstand, I sank back down into my bed and pulled the covers over me. It still smelled like him. Outdoorsy, crisp, clean, and like the open water. Damn him for his lingering scent. Damn him for being right there while I was in a vulnerable state and damn him for wanting to kiss me. If he wanted to kiss me again, I'd let him because I knew damn well what that kiss would lead to, and now that I'd experienced him, my body wanted more and possibly needed more. I took in a deep breath as I closed my eyes.

CHAPTER 15

Fiona

I poured some coffee in my travel mug, grabbed my purse, hopped into my car, and headed to Paso Robles. My eyes were shielded by my sunglasses as the sun was at full force and shining brightly amongst the thin scattered clouds that graced the blue sky. The warm wind blew across my face and my favorite tunes were on full blast. It was a beautiful California day for a road trip, one that I hoped would be worth it. As I was driving on the 101, singing along to Meghan Trainor's "No," my phone rang and Nathan's name popped up.

"Good morning, Nathan," I answered.

"Good morning. I'm thinking breakfast. What do you say?"

"No can do."

"Excuse me?" he spoke with a hint of irritation in his voice.

"I'm on the road and I won't be back until early evening."

"Where are you going?"

"To the vineyard in Paso Robles."

"That's a three-and-a-half-hour drive."

"I know that."

"Why didn't you tell me this yesterday? You could have taken my plane and been there in an hour."

"I like the drive. It clears my head. Plus, why would I tell you?"

I heard a long sigh. "Because I'm an investor and I think I have a right to know."

"You're not an investor yet. I haven't seen any proposals."

"That's because every time I try to get with you, you're unavailable!" he shouted.

I smiled.

"Have to go, Nathan. Josh is calling in. Talk to you soon. Have a good day."

I turned up the radio and leaned back in my seat. Josh didn't call. I just wasn't about to sit and listen to Nathan shout at me.

Nathan

Damn her! "Kylie," I shouted.

"Yes, Nathan?"

"Find out which vineyard Winslow Wines uses in Paso Robles and call my pilot and have him get the plane ready."

"Yes, sir." She walked out of my office.

When I told Fiona that maybe I needed her last night, I wasn't lying. I did need her. I needed to have sex with her again. The other night was incredible and she left me wanting more of her. I could still smell her scent. A mixture of lilies and roses. A perfume that I found extremely sexy, and one my cock also enjoyed.

"Excuse me, Nathan?" Kylie popped her head into my office.

"What did you find out?"

"Winslow Wines gets their grapes from Tobias Vineyards. Your pilot is on standby whenever you're ready."

"Excellent. Tell him I'll be there in about an hour. I should arrive about the same time as Fiona."

"Will do. You have a meeting with Paulie Sands today at three o'clock."

"Cancel it. I won't be back in time. In fact, I won't be back until this evening."

"Shall I cancel your dinner plans with Michelle?"

"Shit. Was that for tonight? Cancel it."

After Kylie walked out, I finished looking over some business reports and my phone beeped with a text message from Michelle.

"Thanks for canceling again, Nathan. I've only seen you once in the past month. Don't bother calling me or setting up another date because it isn't going to happen."

"That's fine, Michelle. See you around."

"Asshole!"

If I had a dollar for every woman that called me an asshole, I'd be a million dollars richer. Oh well, there was only one woman I was interested in at the moment and I wasn't going to stand for her telling me no anymore.

Fiona

I finally arrived at Tobias Vineyards. After driving about a half a mile in, I parked the car outside of the office building and went inside.

"May I help you?" the redhead behind the desk asked.

I sighed as I stared at her. "I'm Fiona Winslow and I'm here to see Ken Raines."

"He's in a meeting at the moment. Please have a seat and as soon as he's finished, I'll let him know you're here." She smiled as she looked at her computer. "I'm sorry, what did you say your name was?"

"Fiona Winslow."

"I don't see you on the schedule for today."

"I didn't make an appointment. Let's call it a surprise visit." I winked.

"Oh. I'll let him know you're here, but he's a very busy man."

"And I'm a very busy woman. Thank you." I smiled as I took a seat in one of the uncomfortable bright blue chairs.

As I was texting Lydia to make sure she was okay, the door opened and I caught a whiff of a scent that was all too familiar to me. Looking up from my phone, my jaw dropped when I saw Nathan standing there smirking at me.

"What the hell are you doing here?" I spoke in a low and irritated voice.

"I figured since you couldn't be in Los Angeles for breakfast or lunch, I'd come to you." He took a seat next to me.

"You need to leave. I have a business meeting."

"I can join you since my company will be investing in yours." He smiled.

"I didn't agree to that yet, and no, you are not joining me."

"Why not? I may be able to help you out."

"I don't need your help, Nathan," I grumbled. Taking in a deep calming breath, I spoke, "Okay, if you leave, I promise we can have lunch together."

"I'm here now, so I might as well stay. And by the way, I will be driving back with you. My pilot had to go back to Los Angeles."

"You're kidding, right?" I frowned.

"No." He smiled.

Damn him and his smile. Once again, his scent was infiltrating my senses and creating that unbearable ache between my legs.

"Excuse me, Miss Winslow?" A tall and handsome older man approached me.

"Yes. Mr. Raines, I presume?" I stood up and held out my hand.

"You can call me Ken." He looked over at Nathan. "Mr. Carter. It's nice to meet you." He held his hand out to him.

"The pleasure is mine, Ken. And please call me Nathan."

"Do the two of you know each other?" I arched my brow.

"No." Ken smiled. "I know *of* Nathan. Please step into my office."

"You stay!" I spoke through gritted teeth at Nathan as I pointed at him.

The corners of his mouth curved up into a sexy smile. "I'm not a dog, Fiona, and I don't take commands from others. Let's not keep Mr. Raines waiting." He placed his hand on the small of my back.

I stiffened as my heels clanked against the tile in a fury of madness.

"I'm sorry to hear about your father. I know his passing was sudden."

"Thank you," I spoke as I took a seat across from Ken's desk and Nathan took the seat beside me.

"Now what brings you here?" He folded his hands.

"I would like to know what's going on with the grapes."

"You know we're in the middle of a drought and we had to raise our prices in order to maintain the grapes' qualities, which included hiring additional staff and putting in new systems."

"I understand that. But I was told that the quality of the grapes had significantly dropped, which in turn was causing delays in the production of our wine."

His eyebrows furrowed at me as he leaned back in his chair.

"The quality of our grapes is the same if not better since using our new system. The reason there's been a delay in the production of your wine is because your company is in debt with us for over two million dollars."

"What?!" I exclaimed.

"You didn't know that?"

"No. I didn't."

"Your father hasn't paid us in a long time. He would come in here begging for extensions, and after doing business with him for twenty-five years, I gave him what he asked, thinking that he was just going through a dry spell and he'd have the money to pay us. But he never did, so we had to cut him off. I even put him on a payment plan, but he failed to make those payments. In fact, we're in the process of suing Winslow Wines, and Christopher was aware of this right before his death. I'll be honest with you, Fiona, your father was a changed man the past couple of years and not in a good way."

"If the debt was repaid immediately, would you begin shipping out the grapes to the winery facility?" Nathan asked.

"Of course. We're a company as well and we just can't carry our clients. We had no choice."

"Can you give me a second? I need to make a phone call." I politely smiled as I walked out of his office.

Pulling my phone from my purse, I dialed Uncle Robbie.

"Hello."

"It's me!" I spoke in anger. "I'm in Paso Robles right now meeting with Ken Raines. Why didn't you tell me that Winslow Wines was in debt with them for over two million dollars?"

"I didn't know we were."

"How could you not! You're the financial manager!" I shouted as the redhead stared at me.

"Fiona, your father told me that he had personally taken care of it and not to record it in the company books."

"And you believed him?"

"Of course I did. I had no reason not to."

"Ugh. Well, he lied. We need to pay Tobias if we want our grapes back."

"We can't right now. We're barely making payroll."

"Then you better find a way! We can't run a wine business without the grapes to make the wine!" I continued to shout.

"You saw the books, Fiona. What the hell do you want me to do? This is why we need Nathan Carter on board. He can supply us with the funds we need to get this company back on track."

"Goodbye, Uncle Robbie." *Click.*

I stood there for a moment, took in a couple deep breaths, and walked back into Ken's office.

"Everything okay?" Nathan asked.

"Yes."

"I'm sorry, but there's nothing left to discuss. Pay us the money your company owes and we'll drop the lawsuit and continue doing business with you. Can I make a suggestion?" he asked.

"Sure. Why not?" I pursed my lips together.

"Winslow Wines is a mess and you seem like a nice person. Don't get caught up in the bad decisions your father made. Maybe it would be in your best interest to get out while you can."

"Thank you for your suggestion, Mr. Raines, but nobody decides what's in my best interest except for me, and maybe this vineyard isn't the one Winslow Wines wants to do business with anymore."

"No skin off my back. You're two million in the hole with us and that's something we don't take lightly. Good luck finding another vineyard because Winslow Wines has made a name for itself and not a good one."

"And I'll be laughing all the way to the bank when Winslow Wines makes a comeback stronger than ever before. Too bad your vineyard won't be associated with our wines. Think of how much business that would drum up for you with other wine companies. Good day, Mr. Raines." I turned on my heels and walked out of his office.

CHAPTER 16

*N*athan

And that was one of the reasons why I came to Paso Robles. Not only to see her, but to see her in action; in business mode. To find out exactly whom I was dealing with. She was tough and she was fierce; two qualities in a woman I never experienced before but found myself turned on by it. I could tell she was pissed by the way she stomped out of the building, holding on to the strap of her purse with a tight grip.

"Who the hell does he think he is, telling me to get out while I can?" She spun around and pointed her finger at me. "Like he's some kind of sexist pig thinking that a woman can't run a company. I can run my father's company." She shook her finger at me. "I can and I will. And when Winslow Wines makes a comeback, I'll come back here and tell him to kiss my ass!"

I stood there with my hands tucked into my pockets and let her rant. She was just as beautiful when she was angry as she was when she wasn't.

"Are you finished?" I smirked.

She looked up at the sky and then back at me. "Yes. Now let's go to lunch."

I wasn't too sure that now was a good time to show her my proposal. That would have to wait until later. Much later, after I fucked her and made her forget about Tobias Vineyards.

"I'll drive." I smiled as I walked over to the driver's side of her car.

Her eyebrow raised at me as she held the keys tightly in her hand.

"No. I'll drive. This is my car and I'm the only one who drives it."

"I'm not a fan of sitting in the passenger's seat."

"Then sit in the back and pretend I'm Jason." She smirked.

"Seriously, Fiona, hand over the keys." I held out my hand.

She glared at me for a moment as if she was trying to figure something out.

"You're a control freak."

"Maybe."

"Well, Mr. Carter, this is one situation you can't control." She opened the driver's side door, climbed in, and started the car. "Are you getting in?" she yelled out the window.

"If I can drive."

"Guess you'll have to call your pilot to take you back to Los Angeles." She began to pull away.

"Fiona Winslow!" I yelled as I headed towards her car.

She stopped and I climbed in, slamming the door shut. She let out a light laugh and took off.

&

Fiona

He held on as if I was going kill him or something.

"Where do you want to go to lunch?" I asked.

"There's this great restaurant called Artisan on 12th and Pine."

"Okay. Artisan it is. Do you know how to get there?" I asked as I put on my sunglasses.

"Just keep taking this road and I'll guide you from there." He sighed.

I could tell he was uncomfortable with me driving, so I slowed down to 20 mph.

"Why are you going so slow?" he asked with an irritated tone.

"Because I'm a scary driver, so I'm trying to ease your fear." I smiled as I looked over at him.

"You are not a scary driver. It's just that I like to drive."

"No. You like to be in control. Admit it."

"Fine. I like to be in control. Make a left at that light up there."

"Yes, sir!" I saluted him.

"And also I don't like to be told 'no' to things. You should know that about me by now. I have a problem with that word."

I rolled my eyes, hit play on my phone, and Meghan Trainor's song "No" came on.

"My name is no. My sign is no. My number is no. You need to let it go. You need to let it go. Nah to the ah, to the no, no, no," I sang as I pointed my finger at him.

He reached over, turned the volume off, and shook his head.

"What the fuck, Fiona?"

I couldn't control the laughter that escaped me. He was pissed and yet so sexy.

"Make a right at the stop sign and the restaurant is on the left." He scowled.

"Oh, come on, Nathan. Where's your fun?"

"Do you have a split personality or something?" he asked.

"What? Why would you ask that?"

"Because just a little while ago, you were mad as hell and now you're singing and laughing."

I shrugged.

After I pulled into the restaurant's parking lot, we got out, and I threw him the keys.

"Catch." I smiled.

"What are you doing?"

"I'm tired. You can drive back to Los Angeles."

The corners of his mouth curved up into a smile as he put my keys in his pocket.

"I still can't believe you came here," I spoke as I sipped on my margarita.

"I wanted to see you."

"You could have waited until I got back."

"Perhaps, but I didn't want to wait." He smirked as he sipped his scotch.

He was intoxicating as he sat across from me. An intoxicating control freak.

"Tell me about you," I spoke.

"There's not much to tell. I pretty much told you everything the other night at dinner."

"You never mentioned your mom."

"She died when I was three, so I don't really remember her."

"I'm sorry, Nathan."

"She died during childbirth and so did my sister."

I swallowed hard, for I didn't know what to say. Hearing something like that so tragic broke my heart.

"I'm so sorry." I reached over and placed my hand on his.

"That was a long time ago."

"So it was just you and your dad or did he re-marry?"

"He never remarried. He just brought home one woman after another. Nothing ever lasted too long. Maybe a couple of weeks, a month. When one woman walked out the door, another walked in."

"Oh," I spoke with a twisted face. I didn't know what to say, so I decided to change the subject. "Now, how about that business proposal?"

He gave a small smile as the waitress set our plates in front of us. "We'll get to that later."

As we were eating, my phone rang. Pulling it from my purse, I saw it was Josh.

"Hello, Josh."

"Fiona, we need to talk, but not over the phone or at the office."

"About what?"

"When will you be home?"

"Not until later. I'm still in Paso Robles."

"I'll stop by your house tomorrow morning around seven."

"What's going on?"

"It's just something I need to discuss with you."

"Okay. I'll see you in the morning."

I ended the call and placed my phone back in my purse.

"Everything okay?" Nathan asked.

"Josh says he needs to talk to me about something. God, I hope he's not quitting."

"Why would he quit?"

"Judging by the status of Winslow Wines, would you want to stay?" I grinned.

His brow arched and a small smile graced his face as he sipped on his drink.

After we finished eating, we hopped into my car and headed back to Los Angeles.

"So, since we're in this car together for the next three and a half to four hours, how about we talk business?" I spoke as I looked over and admired how hot he looked driving my car. He was leaned back in the seat, one hand on the steering wheel and the other resting on his lap.

"We will in time." He smirked as he looked over at me.

"Why not now?"

"Because I said so."

Rolling my eyes, I looked out the passenger window. What was he up to? Why the hesitation to talk about it now?

CHAPTER 17

*F*iona

Nathan pulled into the winding driveway of his Malibu home, which sprawled out over an acre. I would classify it as a modern elegance resort-style home. If the outside was this beautiful, I couldn't wait to see the inside.

Nathan got out of the car, walked over, and opened the door for me.

"Thank you." I smiled.

"You're welcome. Would you like to see my home? Maybe have a drink?"

"I would."

I knew all too well what was going to happen. We'd be having sex in a matter of minutes. Was it wrong? Perhaps. But my body didn't care. I wanted to feel him all over me again. The desire was too strong to deny.

I followed him inside his five-thousand-square-foot single-story beach house and instantly fell in love. From the open floor plan, the sea stone floors throughout, the floor-to-ceiling windows that overlooked the ocean, and the Italian marble floor to ceiling fireplace had me hooked.

"Wow. This is beautiful."

"Thank you." He smiled.

"Did you decorate it yourself?" I asked as I followed him to the kitchen.

"No. I had an interior designer come in and decorate the place for me. Vodka on the rocks?" he asked.

"Sounds good."

While he was pouring our drinks, I stepped outside on the patio and gasped when I saw the large in-ground pool that was almost the length of the house. At one end of the pool, there was a fireplace with a loveseat and a couple of chairs in front of it surrounded by Italian marble with recessed lights and a bar over to the left.

"Your drink." Nathan smiled as he handed it to me.

"Thank you. This is some pool. My God, it's huge."

He chuckled. "It's one of the best features of the house. I swim every day. Maybe one day, you'd like to join me." He winked.

I gave him a small smile as I sipped my vodka.

"Why don't we go inside?" He lightly placed his hand on my back.

Walking back inside the house, Nathan took my drink from my hand and set it down. Our eyes locked onto each other as his fingers began to slowly unbutton my blouse.

"I've been wanting you all day. I hope you don't mind." His lips pressed against mine.

"No. Not at all," I whispered as our kiss deepened.

His fingers deftly slid my blouse off my shoulders, sending it to the ground. Breaking our kiss, he reached behind and unhooked my bra, exposing my breasts. The hunger in his eyes grew as he lightly traced his finger over each one, caressing them softly before taking each hardened peak in between his fingers. The bulge in his pants grew quickly. Knowing that I turned him on so much caused an explosion inside me, intensifying the deep and uncontrollable ache between my legs. Taking his hand, I placed it up my skirt, begging for his touch. The corners of his mouth curved up into a smile as his eyes stared into mine.

"Is that what you want? You want my fingers inside your wet and warm pussy?" he whispered in my ear.

"Yes," I replied with bated breath.

"Do you want me to make you come?" His lips swept over my neck.

"Yes."

Pushing the fabric of my panties to the side, he plunged a finger inside me without hesitation. I gasped and a low growl rumbled in his chest. I needed to feel his cock in my hand. I was horny as hell and I wasn't holding back. His lips glided across my throat and down my chest, while his tongue circled around my nipple. Unbuckling his belt, I forcefully took down his pants and wrapped my hand around his cock. The moan that erupted from him excited me even more. He continued to suck each breast as his finger moved in and out of me, stimulating me in a way that threw my body into a rapid orgasm. I moaned and threw my head back as he held my body against him with one hand.

"That's it. Come for me, beautiful."

He removed his finger from me and my hand from his cock. Reaching back, he unzipped my skirt, letting it fall to the floor.

"Leave your heels on." He smiled.

"Are you going to show me your bedroom?" I asked breathlessly, still trying to recover from my orgasm.

"No. I'm going to show you my dining room table."

He kicked off his shoes and stepped out of his pants before taking my hand and leading me to the table. Picking me up, he placed me on it, took a step back, and stared at me while taking off his shirt. His eyes raked over my entire body. No one had ever looked at me that way before, including John. His desire for me was obvious, just as mine was for him.

"Spread your legs and bring them up on the table," he commanded as he walked over to me.

Doing as he asked, he licked up the inside of my thigh while his fingers hooked into the sides of my panties. Lifting my ass from the table, he removed them and tossed them to the floor while his tongue explored me.

"You taste so damn good, Fiona."

My hands stayed firmly planted on the table as his mouth covered me, causing me to let out sounds I never knew existed. It felt so good. He felt so good. His tongue slid up my torso as his fingers dipped inside me. Taking my breast in his mouth, he moaned.

"I could suck these beautiful tits all day and all night."

His finger moved rapidly inside me as I swelled against him. It was happening again. Another orgasm was coming. He felt it as he leaned over me and stared into my eyes with a smile splayed across his face.

"You're so easy to make come. Do you have any clue how much that turns me on?"

"You turn me on," I whispered as I brought one hand to his cheek and my body gave in, releasing itself to him.

"That's it. Look into my eyes as you come, beautiful. I want to see that mind-blowing expression on your face."

Placing his hands on my hips, he lifted me from the table and turned me around, bending me over so he could take me from behind. I was caught up in the heat of the moment and I welcomed any position he wanted. So caught up, I didn't hear the sound of the condom wrapper. He stood behind me and cupped my ass firmly with his hands before thrusting inside of me, hard and deep as he moaned with each thrust. His fingers pressed tightly into my hips as he moved in and out of me at a rapid pace. His moans grew louder as the warmth and wetness inside me enveloped around his hard cock. Orgasm number three was on its way and had me in such a hold that I forgot for a moment where I was. His hand reached in front me and he pressed his fingers against my clit, intensifying the orgasm that had already emerged. My legs tightened and my body shook as he slowed down and pushed deep inside me, releasing himself.

"Ah," he moaned. "Oh my God."

My heart was rapidly beating as I stood there while he was still buried inside me, trying to catch his breath. Before he pulled out, he softly kissed my back.

"Stay right here and I'll get you a towel to clean yourself with."

I turned around and leaned against the table, my body still on fire.

I watched as Nathan walked his naked, strong, and ripped body towards me with a small towel in his hand.

"Here you go."

"Thanks."

As I cleaned myself up, he slipped into his pants.

"Another vodka on the rocks?" he asked.

"No thanks," I replied as I picked up my clothes off the floor. "Where's the bathroom?"

"Down that hallway and first door on the left."

When I entered the bathroom, I closed the door and fell back against it. Something happened to me and I couldn't quite describe it. *Fuck. Fuck. Fuck.* I lightly tapped my head against the door. I was falling for him and I was falling hard. *Shit. No!* I couldn't and I wouldn't. I didn't trust him or any man, for that matter. This was a game. A corporate game. Sex. Only sex. I needed to get out of here, but first I needed to compose myself. After getting myself dressed, I calmly and casually walked to the living room and grabbed my purse.

"Thank you," I shouted as I walked towards the front door.

"Wait," Nathan spoke as he emerged from the kitchen. "Are you sure you don't want another drink?"

"I'm sure and I need to leave. But first, why don't you give me the business proposal to look over tonight?"

"It can wait until tomorrow." He kissed my forehead. "Be careful driving home and when you arrive, send me a text."

"Why?" I asked with a raised brow.

"So I know you made it home safe."

I could feel myself choking up inside. No man had ever asked me to text him when I got home.

"Oh, okay." I gave a small smile.

He placed his hand on my cheek before I walked out the door.

"I had a lot of fun today. Let's do it again."

"Me too." I placed my hand on his chest. "Have a good night, Nathan."

"You too, Fiona. Don't forget to text me."

"I won't." I turned around and spoke before heading to my car.

CHAPTER 18

*N*athan

I shut the door and walked into my office, taking the proposal from my desk and looking at it. There was a feeling inside me. One I didn't like. One that sent me into a state of confusion. This was a business deal and a business deal only. Regardless of my feelings for her, it was a deal that needed to be made. It was nothing personal. But why did I find myself hesitant to show her? Throwing the proposal down on my desk, I went and took a shower. After wrapping a towel around my waist, I checked my phone to see if she texted me. She didn't. Looking at the time, she should have been home by now. I'd give her a few more minutes before texting her. I dried myself off, put on a pair of pajama bottoms, and climbed into bed. Still, no text.

"Are you home?" I abruptly typed with aggravation that she couldn't do one simple thing I asked.

"Oh. Sorry. I forgot to text you. Yes, I'm home."

She forgot? How the fuck could she forget?

"I asked you to text me. How could you forget?"

"Were you worried about me or something? Are you questioning my driving abilities?"

Smart ass.

"No. I wasn't worried. It's the point that I asked you to do something and you didn't do it. How am I supposed to trust that you'd turn your company around with my money if you can't follow a simple request?"

"Are you finished? I'm tired and Josh will be here at seven. Good night, Nathan. I'm home, I'm safe, and I'm fine."

"Good night."

How dare she talk to me that way? Setting my phone down, I lay my head on my pillow and sighed. I tossed and turned a few times, trying to calm my racing mind. Bolting back up, I grabbed my phone.

"One simple request, Fiona. One simple request."

"Go to sleep, Nathan."

The next morning, I was sitting at my desk looking out at the magnificent city of Los Angeles when Will walked into my office.

"How did it go yesterday? Did you get her to sign?"

Turning my chair around, I took a sip of my coffee before answering him.

"I haven't shown her yet."

"What? Why? What are you waiting for?"

"Maybe we need to revise the proposal."

"No way, Nathan. It's what's best for the company and your money."

I sighed.

"Wait a minute. Hold on a second." He pointed his finger at me. "Do you have feelings for her? Are you letting personal feelings get in the way of business?"

"No. It's just I saw her yesterday in action with Ken Raines. She's tough and I think she can handle the company on her own."

"Oh, so you sat in on one meeting and now you think she's capable? With your money? What the hell, Nathan? What's your number one rule? The one you've stuck by for years? Never let personal feelings interfere with business. Always keep the two separate."

"I know." I let out a deep sigh. "You're right. I'll see her today and give her the proposal."

"I'll come with you," he spoke.

"No need. I'm handling this one on my own."

"Just make sure you don't let your dick rule."

"Have I ever?" I cocked my head.

"Just making sure." He winked as he left my office.

Fiona

Pouring two cups of coffee, I took them over to the table where Josh was sitting.

"Nice house."

"Thanks. Now what brings you here at seven a.m.?" I asked as I sat down.

He took a sip from his cup and then set it down. "I stumbled upon something yesterday and it freaked me out."

"What was it?" I held my cup between my hands.

"Your father was stealing money from the employee pension."

"What? How do you—"

He quickly pulled some papers from his brown leather bag and handed them to me.

"Serena, the woman that works in the production department asked your uncle for her pension statement because she hadn't received one in a long time. Robbie pulled one for her and she took it home to her husband, who ran some numbers that didn't add up. When she confronted your uncle about it, he said there was a problem with the computer system a while back and it probably didn't update and he'd look into it. So, I started digging around myself. I hope you don't mind."

"No. Not at all. I think." I bit down on my bottom lip.

"All of the money that was taken from the employees' checks to be put into their pension fund went into another account, which was used for company operations."

"Shit." I shook my head. "How much are we talking?"

He pursed his lips and stared at me.

"Josh. How much?"

"Over fifteen million dollars."

"What?" I accidentally knocked over my coffee cup.

Josh got up and grabbed the roll of paper towel that was sitting on the counter.

"That was my reaction minus the spilling of coffee."

"And you're saying my uncle knew about this?"

"Yeah, Fiona. I'm sorry."

As Josh cleaned up my mess, I covered my face with my hands. I was in shock, disbelief, and I was pissed.

"How could my father do that?"

"I don't know. I didn't know him that well."

"Oh my God, Josh. Does anyone else know about this?"

"No. Just us. I would never say a word to anyone. That's why I didn't want to talk about this at the office. What are you going to do, Fiona? You could go to jail."

"Me!" I exclaimed. "I had nothing to do with this."

"I know, but you're the CEO now and you're his daughter." He looked at his watch. "I better get to the office before someone starts asking where I am. I'm sorry, Fiona."

"Thanks, Josh. You did the right thing by telling me. But I want to make one thing very clear to you. You know nothing about this. Understand?"

"Yeah. I understand. I'll see you at the office."

After Josh left, I poured the rest of the coffee into my travel mug, grabbed my purse, and drove to the office. A feeling of hurt and betrayal coursed through my veins. How could my father do what he did? How could he steal from the employees that worked for him for so many years? There was only one person who could answer my questions and that was my Uncle Robbie.

I stormed down the hallway to his office. The clanking of my heels against the cold tile could be heard throughout the building. Opening the door to his office without even knocking, I stepped inside and threw down my purse.

"Fiona, what's going on?"

"How could you not tell me that my father stole from the company pension fund?" I spoke through gritted teeth as my finger angrily pointed at him.

He put his hands up. "I was going to tell you."

"When?!" I demanded to know.

"Sit down."

"NO! I am not sitting down and I want some answers NOW!"

"Your father said he had a plan to put the money back, but unfortunately, he died before he told me what that plan was."

"How could you let him do it?" I asked as I stood there with my arms folded, shaking my head.

"Your father was desperate to try and save this company. He misused the company's pension on a bad business deal, which sent this company and all of us down the rabbit hole. There was nothing I could do to stop him."

"UGH!" I yelled as I paced around the room. "If we don't go to the authorities about this, we'll go to jail. Not just me, but you!" I pointed at him.

"And that is why we have to get that money back into the pension fund. It's the main reason we need Nathan Carter."

"You think Nathan Carter is going to want anything to do with this company once he finds out that my father stole the pension funds?"

"He doesn't need to know. He'll invest and we'll take the fifteen million dollars and put it back."

"And what about the rest of the money we owe to the creditors? Not to mention the fact that we no longer have a vineyard supplying us grapes. I can understand now why my father had a massive heart attack. Fuck. I'm going to my office. I need to calm down and think." I grabbed my purse and walked out.

CHAPTER 19

*F*iona This was a nightmare. A nightmare that was never ending and one I couldn't wake up from. As I took a seat behind my desk, my phone began to ring.

"Hey, Lydia." I sighed.

"Are you okay?"

"No. Actually, I'm not."

"Business?"

"As always."

"I was hoping you could go with me Monday to my first doctor's appointment. I'm a little nervous and I need my best friend with me."

"Of course I'll go. What time is your appointment?"

"Eight o'clock."

"I'll pencil you in."

"Thanks, Fiona. I love you."

"I love you too."

Just as I ended the call, I looked up to see Nathan leaning against the doorframe of my office. *Crap.* He was so sexy, but I couldn't deal with him right now.

"I love you?" His brow arched.

"I was talking to Lydia."

"Are the two of you in some sort of relationship I should know about?" He smirked.

Bringing my forehead to my hand, I spoke, "We're having a baby."

"What?" he exclaimed as he stepped inside.

"I mean; she's having a baby. But she's like a sister to me, so we're having a baby."

"What about the father?"

"He's a lying scumbag who wasn't even from L.A. He lied to her, and then left and deleted his profile. Typical man."

"How did they meet?"

"Tinder." I rolled my eyes.

"Well, there you have it. Tinder men are all lying scumbags."

"Correction, all men are as far as I'm concerned. Tinder or no Tinder."

He looked at me with narrowed eyes. "What's wrong? You're in a mood."

"Nothing." I sighed. "Just another clusterfuck of a day at Winslow Wines."

He looked at his Rolex. "The day just started."

"And?" I arched my brow. "What are you doing here?"

"I bring to you my business proposal and the solution to all of your problems so you won't continue to have clusterfuck days here at Winslow Wines." He handed me a large envelope. "Look it over later when you have a clear head."

"Thanks, Nathan."

"You're welcome. I have to go. I have a meeting to get to." He walked over, kissed my forehead, and left.

The touch of his lips against my skin sent riveting pulses throughout my body. Seeing him in his designer suit, looking all handsome and sexy, made my day a little brighter. For a second, I forgot that my father stole the money from the employees' pension fund.

"UGH!" I placed my hand on each side of my head.

"Fiona, are you okay?" Josh asked as he walked in.

"No. No I'm not okay, Josh. You know why I'm not okay. Do I look okay? I'm stressed. I could go to jail. This company could be shut down in a split second and I don't know what to do!" I yelled.

"Calm down. You can't make rational decisions by being so upset. Listen, take the rest of the day off. Go somewhere quiet where you can think."

"Good idea." I pointed at him as I grabbed my purse and the envelope Nathan handed me. "If anyone asks, I wasn't feeling well." I walked out and headed to my car.

As I climbed in and held the envelope in my hands, I decided just to look it over really quick to get an idea of what he was proposing. Pulling the thick stack of white papers out, I scanned the first few lines and nearly stopped breathing. Was he serious? Oh hell no! I punched in his building address on my GPS and headed straight to his office. Taking the elevator to the tenth floor, I stepped out and looked around.

"Excuse me," I spoke as I stopped a nice-looking man in the hallway. "Where can I find Nathan Carter's office?"

"Keep going straight and make a right. You'll see his secretary sitting at her desk. She's the redhead."

Of course she was.

I approached her desk and looked at the nameplate that was sitting proud and center on the desk.

"Hello, Belinda. Is he in there?"

"Yes, but he's—"

I didn't wait for her to finish her sentence as I abruptly opened the door to find him and Will sitting at a round glass table.

"Fiona? What the—"

"Really, Nathan? You want to invest in my company and take controlling interest? Are you fucking serious?"

"Calm down." He got up from his chair. "Will, we'll resume this meeting after."

Will got up and gave me a smile. A smile that I wanted to smack right off his face.

"Good to see you, Fiona," he spoke as he walked past me and out the door.

"Have a seat," Nathan spoke as he pulled out a chair for me.

"NO! I'm not sitting because I'm not staying. There's nothing to discuss. You are not taking over my company! Investing is one thing, but to take controlling interest is absurd. How the hell do you even have time for that?"

"You need me and the bottom line is I need to do what's best for me and for your company. I'm taking a huge-ass risk. You're on the verge of bankruptcy and shutting down Winslow Wines forever. I'm simply trying to help you. I need to make sure that my money is well invested, and I can do that if I own controlling interest."

"So you don't trust me? You don't think I can bring life back into MY company that MY father left me?"

"Fiona, face it. He left you in the red and with a shitload of troubles. You should consider yourself lucky that I want to step in and help. Not many other businessmen would want to invest in your company right now. And to be honest, you've never run a company before. But don't worry, sweetheart, you'll still be in charge. You'll just have to run all decisions by me first."

"First of all, asshole," I pointed my finger at him, "don't call me sweetheart. And second of all, I don't have to run anything by you because I'm declining your offer." I threw the stack of papers on the table. "I knew you were up to something, but I never thought you'd want to take over. I thought you genuinely cared about helping us, but I was wrong. You're a snake in the grass just like every other asshole man out in the world."

"Ouch." He placed his hand over his heart. "You'll sink without my help. Remember that."

"Then I'll go down with the ship but on my own terms." I turned on my heels and began to walk out.

"By the way," he shouted, "if something happens to my car, I'll know it was you."

"UGH!" I stormed out.

Rage consumed me. It consumed me so badly that I couldn't think clearly or see straight. I needed to go somewhere. Somewhere quiet to process everything that was going on and be alone where I could harvest my inner calm. Little Tokyo was the first place that came to mind. I drove to the Japanese American Cultural and Community center and made my way to the James Irvine Japanese Garden. It wasn't anything big. Just a small garden lined with rocks, flowers, blooming trees, and a stream that flowed from a waterfall. It was the perfect place to sit down, relax, and gather my thoughts. Sitting on a rock, I took in the serene sound of the stream and began to calm down. If I could escape from my life right now and jet off to some island where corporations and asshole men didn't exist, I'd be fine.

"Damn you, Dad, for dying and leaving me with this mess," I spoke as I looked up at the sky. "Why did you do it? Why did you have to steal from your employees?"

Not only did we owe the pension fund fifteen million dollars, we also owed the vineyard two million, not to mention all the other creditors that were knocking on the door. Uncle Robbie told me that a bank loan was out of the question because my father tried a year ago and they turned him down. I was at a loss. With no grapes, there was no wine. No wine meant no sales and no sales meant no money. We'd be forced into bankruptcy, which would raise a red flag concerning the pension fund. An investigation would be launched and I'd be saying hello to my new jail cell.

Nathan and his damn proposal. Motherfucker. He was trying to take the company right out from under me. Swoop in and act like the hero he wasn't. Deals always came with a price. Unfortunately, my price would be losing the company my father started when I was three years old. A company I wanted nothing to do with because I was so angry at him for betraying our family. But now that he was dead and left me in charge, I would have no choice but to make the responsible business decisions that he failed to do.

CHAPTER 20

Nathan

I didn't think my proposal would go over well with her, but I didn't expect her to storm into my office and call me names. Well, maybe I did. Was it wrong that I was turned on the whole time she was yelling at me? Regardless of what my feelings were for her, which, I'm not even really sure what they were, I had to make the best business decision possible.

"So, I take it she hated our proposal," Will spoke as he stepped into my office.

"I guess so." I sighed as I took a seat behind my desk.

"She's a little spitfire, that one." He smiled. "A very sexy little spitfire. I thought you had her under control. Maybe you should have waited until you fucked her a few more times."

"I don't think that would have mattered. She's a strong woman with a strong personality."

"So now what?" he asked.

"Give her some time. Let her calm down. Something was wrong with her when I walked into her office this morning. She was already stressed about something else and I have a feeling it was something serious."

Climbing into the back of the limo after a late meeting with a client, I pulled my phone from my pocket and dialed Fiona's number. She had been on my mind all day and I wanted to make sure she was home and okay.

"Well, look who's calling," she answered. "The great savior Nathan Carter."

"Fiona? Where are you? Are you drunk?"

"Maybe. Slightly," she slurred. "Why are you calling me?"

There were loud voices in the background and music playing. I could barely hear her.

"Are you alone?" I asked.

"What's it to you?"

"Answer the damn question, Fiona."

"Don't use that tone with me, mister. I'm out trying to harness my inner calm," she slurred.

"Where are you?" I asked.

"Where are you? I have to go."

She hung up on me, so I called her again. After the fourth ring, a man's voice answered.

"Hello."

"Who is this?" I asked in an abrupt tone.

"Joey, the bartender. Were you the one she was just talking to?"

"Yes. Where is she?"

"Sitting on a barstool in front of me at the Wolf and Crane Bar in Little Tokyo. She's been here for four hours and she's hammered. I can't let her drive home. Can you pick her up?"

"I'm on my way. Don't let her out of your sight."

"I won't."

"And cut her off."

"I already have, man, and she's not happy."

"I'm sure she's not."

I ended the call and looked at Jason.

"We're going to the Wolf and Crane Bar in Little Tokyo to pick up a very drunk Fiona."

"This should be interesting." He smirked.

Fiona

"Come on, Joey. Fill it up. Please?" I whined as I leaned over the bar.

"Sorry, Fiona. I can't. You've had enough. Listen, getting drunk because you had a bad day isn't going to help you or anything. The only thing that's going to come from this is a really bad headache in the morning and the feeling that you've been hit by a train."

"Then I'm going somewhere else." I haphazardly got up from the stool and fell back down onto it.

"Whoa." Joey grabbed hold of my arm. "Sit tight and I'll bring you another drink. But first, I have to take care of some other customers."

"Okay." I smiled as I laid my head down on the bar.

My head was spinning. The room was spinning and I felt a hand lightly grab hold of my arm. When I lifted my head, I saw Nathan standing there.

"Are you okay?"

"What are you doing here?" I slurred.

"Taking you home. You've had your fill for the night. Come on."

"No!" I jerked my arm from him and fell over on the guy sitting next to me. "Oh, sorry." I looked at him.

Joey walked over and looked at me. "Go home, Fiona, and get some rest."

"How much does she owe?"

"One hundred fifty."

"Jesus, Fiona." Nathan looked at me and pulled out his wallet.

He threw some money on the bar, picked me up from the stool, and carried me to his limo. I was too tired to fight him and, at this point, I didn't care. I just wanted to pass out. He slid in next to me and, instantly, my head fell onto his shoulder.

"I need to lie down," I whispered as I lay my head across his lap.

His fingers brushed my hair from my face.

"You're an asshole," I slurred.

"I know I am." He looked down at me. "Now be quiet and close your eyes."

"Do you know that I hate redheads?"

"Why's that?" he asked.

"My father's mistress was a redhead before she changed her hair color to brown. The woman who John was cheating with on me is a redhead and a redhead got my promotion. Redheads have ruined my life."

He lightly chuckled. "We'll talk about the redheads another time."

The way he was stroking my hair relaxed me as my eyes closed and I attempted to drift into a sound sleep.

Nathan

"Just drive home, Jason. She's too drunk to be left alone."

"Yes, sir."

The only thing I could see as I stroked her soft blonde hair was the silhouette of her beautiful face as the moonlight shined through the window. She didn't get like this just because of my proposal. There had to be something else going on and my proposal sent her over the edge.

Jason opened the door and I climbed out, picked her up, and carried her inside my house. She moaned as her arms wrapped around my neck and her head lay against my chest. Carrying her to the guest bedroom, I lay her down on the bed and removed her shoes. As I was unbuttoning her blouse, I couldn't help but stare down at her beautiful breasts. Her eyes slowly opened and stared at me as she brought her hand to my face.

"Fuck me," she whispered.

"If it were under any other circumstances, I would, but not

tonight, beautiful. You're too drunk and I would never take advantage of you that way."

Her eyes closed and I removed her blouse and pulled off her skirt. Her body was perfection, a wonderland that I was desperate to revisit. My cock was twitching as I stared at her. Sighing, I got up from the bed and went into my room and grabbed a t-shirt. Lifting her up, I slipped it over her head and pulled the covers over her. Before I left, I softly brushed my lips against hers.

"Sleep tight, beautiful."

CHAPTER 21

Fiona

Slowly turning my aching head, I opened my eyes, which felt like they were weighted down by heavy weights. Beige walls, fireplace, wall-mounted TV, two mocha-colored chairs that sat across from a beige-colored sofa, a square glass table and wooden floors were what my eyes saw. This was not my bedroom. Panic struck inside me as I lifted up the crème-colored sheet that covered me and stared at the black t-shirt I was wearing. Where the fuck was I? Oh my God, someone must have slipped me a roofie at the bar last night, brought me to his place, and had sex with me. I reached down and felt my panties were still intact. If we'd had sex, I would be naked, right? People who roofie other people don't just casually dress them afterwards. My pounding head was racing with all sorts of thoughts. I had no memory of last night. The last thing I remembered was sitting on the barstool, telling the bartender about my shitty life and throwing back one drink after another. *Shit*. I couldn't even remember what I was drinking.

I gulped as I slowly sat up. I could smell the aroma of fresh brewed coffee. My stomach churned. I carefully got out of bed and tiptoed to the closed door, leaning my ear against it to see if I could hear someone. Looking over at the two door walls that sat in the corner, I walked over and stared out at the ocean. Wait a minute. This was Nathan's house. Fuck my life. Walking into the bathroom, I stared at myself in the mirror and saw the mascara that was sitting beneath my red swollen eyes. Grabbing a washcloth, I ran it under cool water, soaped it up, and washed my face, hoping that somehow it would make me feel somewhat better. It didn't.

Stepping into the hallway, I went to the kitchen, where I saw Nathan sitting at the island on his laptop.

"Good morning." He turned and looked at me. "I'm sure I don't need to ask how you're feeling."

"No. No, you don't."

"Go sit down outside. The fresh air will help you and I'll bring you some coffee."

"Thanks." My lips gave way to a small smile.

Taking a seat in the lounge chair that faced the sand and the ocean, Nathan handed me a cup of coffee and took a seat next to me.

"How did I get here?" I asked as I slowly sipped from the cup.

"I picked you up and I felt you were too drunk to be home alone, so I brought you here."

"How did you know where I was?"

"You don't remember?" His eye narrowed.

"No."

"I called you and you hung up on me, so I called back and the bartender answered your phone. He told me that I needed to come get you."

"Oh. Thank you."

"You're welcome. Would you like to tell me why you got so inebriated yesterday?"

As I held the cup between my hands, I stared out as the waves crashed against the shoreline.

"I had a shitty day."

"I know you did, but I know you being pissed off about my proposal was only half of it. What else happened?"

I looked over at him. "Did we have sex last night?"

The corners of his mouth slightly curved upwards. "No. Stop changing the subject."

"How did I get in your t-shirt?"

"I took your clothes off and put it on you."

"But we didn't have sex?"

"No. We did not have sex. I wasn't about to take advantage of you when you were so drunk. Now answer my question."

Wow. Nathan Carter had some morals. Who would have thought? I heavily sighed as I stared out at the water.

"My father stole money from the employee pension fund."

"Are you kidding me?"

"I wish I was." I looked over at him.

"How much did he take?"

"Fifteen million dollars."

"Holy shit. Why?"

"The only thing I know is that a business deal went bad. My uncle doesn't know the details because my father wouldn't tell him. He just told him to keep his mouth shut and go on with business as if it never happened. Apparently, my father was working on a plan to put the money back, but he died before he could execute it."

"And your uncle doesn't know what that plan was?"

"No. I had just found that out right before you came to the office with your proposal. Your timing couldn't have been any worse."

"Sorry about that. So, another subject, you hate redheads, eh?"

Narrowing my eyes at him, I spoke, "How do you know that?"

"You told me in the limo last night when your head was in my lap." He smiled.

"Shit. What else did I say?"

"You called me an asshole. That's about it."

"Great." I sat there shaking my head. "I don't apologize for calling you an asshole because you are one."

"I know." He shrugged.

"So back to the redhead hatred." He smirked. "You said that redheads have ruined your life."

"They have." I arched my brow as I took a sip of coffee. "My stepmother, my ex's mistress, and my ex-boss who gave my promotion to the redhead who was sucking his dick."

"The way you say it makes it sound so dirty." He winked.

"Shut up." I laughed as I lightly smacked his arm. "Is it okay if I take a quick shower before I head home? And I need to go get my car."

"Of course it is and your car is already at your house. I had someone pick it up earlier."

"Wow. Thank you, Nathan."

"You're welcome." He got up from his seat. "Hey, I'm attending a cocktail party tonight on a yacht. Would you like to come with me? After all, it is a Saturday and I think you need to take your mind off of Winslow Wines for a couple of days."

"You really want me to go with you, even though I think you're an asshole?"

"A lot of people think I'm an asshole, but it doesn't mean I don't enjoy their company."

"You mean women." I raised my brow.

"Ninety percent of them are women."

"Sounds like fun. I'd love to go." I smiled.

"Good. Now get your hungover ass in the shower." He smirked as he walked away.

I smiled as I finished off the rest of my coffee. Stepping into the shower, I closed my eyes and tilted my head back, letting the hot water soothe my aching head. This showerhead was magical. Way better than the one I had at home. As I was in my zone, feeling completely relaxed without a care in the world at that moment, I heard the shower door open and a fully naked Nathan Carter stepped inside.

"What are you doing?"

"I didn't think you'd mind if I took a shower with you." His lips caressed my neck and, suddenly, I could feel myself melting away.

"And what if I do?"

"Then all you have to say is no. It's simple." His tongue slid down my chest and to each of my breasts. "Are you saying no, Fiona?"

"No. I mean, yes. I mean, no. I'm not saying no." I fumbled with my words because he felt incredible.

"Good, because I've been wanting you since last night." His lips traveled up to mine as his hand cupped me down below.

My hands stayed fixated to his muscular chest as he passionately kissed me. His finger dipped inside me and I let out a gasp as I tilted my head back, taking in the pleasure he provided me. My hand traveled from his chest, down to his rock hard abs, and my fingers traced the sexy v-line that drove me crazy. When I wrapped my hand around his hard cock, he let out a moan as I moved up and down his shaft.

"I want you to get down on your knees and suck me. Can you do that for me?" he asked with a whisper.

Getting on my knees, the hot water beaded down on me as my lips wrapped around the tip of him, lightly sucking before inserting him fully into my mouth. His hands fisted through my hair as he moved my head up and down, forcing me to suck him deeper. I never enjoyed giving a guy a blowjob; in fact, I hated it. But with him, I found myself enjoying it. I wanted to give him the same pleasure he had given me. His moans grew louder as he thrust his hips, then suddenly, he pulled out of my mouth.

"I don't want to come that way. We'll save that for another time. Get up here," he commanded as he brought my leg up to his waist and thrust inside me with force.

"Fuck. You feel so good, baby," he spoke with bated breath as he continued to move in and out of me.

My moans heightened as I swelled around him and my body gave way to an electrifying orgasm. I could feel his cock pulsating inside me as I came. He pulled out, wrapped his hand around himself, and finished himself off on my stomach. Watching him do that was the sexiest thing I'd ever seen. He wasn't the first guy to jack himself off in front of me, but he sure was the sexiest one. Once he was finished, he placed his hands on each side of my face and his mouth smashed into mine.

"I didn't come in you because I wasn't wearing a condom and I didn't know if you were on birth control," he spoke breathlessly.

"I am on birth control."

He gave me a small smile as his hands ran down wet hair. Once we finished our shower, he got out first and handed me a towel. He went to his room to get dressed while I finished drying off and slipped back into my clothes from last night.

"Jason is going to drive you home and then I'll have him pick you up at six o'clock and bring you to the yacht."

"You're not coming to pick me up?" I asked.

"No. I'll meet you there." He placed his thumb on my chin and softly kissed my lips.

CHAPTER 22

Fiona

As soon as I walked through the door, I called Lydia and asked her to come over. So many feelings and emotions were running through my head where Nathan and the company were concerned and I needed my best friend.

"I was going to call you last night, but I was on skype with my parents for two hours and then I was so tired, I crashed."

"Did you tell them about the baby?" I asked as I made her some tea.

"Yeah and they say they're happy, but I got the feeling they really weren't."

"They're happy, Lydia. They're just worried about you being a single mom."

"Maybe. So what did you do last night? Anything exciting?"

"We have so much to talk about." I took a seat next to her on the couch and brought up my legs. "First of all, I found out my father stole from the employees' pension fund."

"What?!" she exclaimed. "Oh my God."

"I know. Second of all, Nathan handed me his business proposal and it turns out he wants to take controlling interest, meaning he'd be in charge of Winslow Wines."

"What a dick. You told him to shove it up his ass, right?"

"Yeah. I did. But then I went to Little Tokyo and did some thinking at the Japanese garden. Then I went and sat in a bar for four hours, poured my heart out to the hot bartender, and then drank myself into oblivion. Nathan came and picked me up, took me back to his place, put me to bed, and then we had shower sex this morning." My teeth bit into my bottom lip.

"Wait a minute." She shook her head. "You had sex with the man who wants to take over your company? Even after you found out he wanted to take over?"

"Yeah." I continued to bite down on my lip.

"What the hell is the matter with you?"

"I know. I'm an idiot, and tonight I'm attending a cocktail party with him on a yacht."

"Fiona, have you fallen for him?"

"I don't know. Maybe."

"He's every kind of wrong for you. You don't trust guys as it is and Nathan Carter is one that shouldn't be trusted."

"I know that and I'm trying so hard to stop my feelings. He's just so damn sexy in everything he does."

"So you're thinking with your vagina instead of your head?"

"No. Of course not."

"Yes you are! Listen to yourself. He's sexy, I get it. He's more than a god in the bedroom and he makes you feel good. But, Fiona, he wants to take over your family business. Did you ever stop to think that getting you into bed with him was a way to make that happen? That he'd sweep you off your feet and get you to sign that proposal? He's a womanizing Casanova."

I rolled my eyes at her, but she was right. He was the hunter and I was his prey, and if I wasn't careful, I'd fall in his trap and my life would forever be changed.

"Don't worry. I know what I'm doing," I spoke.

"I think you're playing a very dangerous game, Fiona, and the last thing I want is for you to get hurt."

"I'm not going to allow myself to get hurt. Now, I have to get ready for the party. Are you staying?"

"I guess." She pouted.

☙

Nathan

Being with Fiona this morning was nice and seeing her in nothing but my t-shirt was hot. I normally didn't like company first thing in the morning but having her in my home and having coffee with me made me feel—good. *Fuck.* I already missed her and her smart mouth. I never missed someone before and I never really gave anyone a second thought, but I found myself thinking about her more than I should have. It wasn't just her body I was obsessed with and couldn't seem to get enough of; it was also her mind, her personality, and her attitude. I'd been with countless women over the years and no one had ever captured my attention the way she had. Normally, I wouldn't give a shit if a woman got drunk. If they called me, I'd send Jason to pick them up and take them home. But with Fiona, I needed to get her myself. I wanted to rescue her and take care of her, which scared the living hell out of me.

After we pulled up to the marina, I sent Jason to pick up Fiona while I made my rounds to all the guests. Music was playing, drinks and appetizers were being served, and people were mingling. As I was socializing, my phone beeped with a text message.

"Fiona has arrived."

"Thank you, Jason."

Making my way through the crowd and down to the entrance of the yacht, I stopped when I saw her. She was gorgeous in her short lace, form-fitting, black strapless dress with stiletto heels to match. Her long blonde hair swept to one side with a cascade of curls. She was simply stunning and the most beautiful woman here. In fact, she was the most beautiful woman in the world as far as I was concerned.

"Good evening, Mr. Carter." She smiled as she approached me.

Taking hold of her hand, I brought it up to my lips.

"Good evening, Miss Winslow. Thank you for coming."

"This is quite a turn out," she spoke as she looked around. "Whose party is this anyway?"

The corners of my mouth curved upwards. "It's my party."

"Your party?"

"Yes. Welcome to my yacht."

"Why didn't you mention that earlier?" She arched her brow.

"I wanted to surprise you."

"I hate surprises."

"I'll have to remember that." I winked as I escorted her onto the boat.

CHAPTER 23

*F*iona

His yacht and his party? Wow. I was impressed. As a waiter walked by with a tray of champagne, Nathan grabbed a glass and handed it to me.

"Not too much of this. I don't want a repeat of last night." He smirked.

"No worries. I don't either. I'm still feeling the effects."

There had to be at least two hundred people on the boat; dancing, holding conversations, laughing, and drinking. This crowd was the upper class if I ever saw one. Men were dressed in their finest suits and tuxedos, and the women, let's just say I'd never seen so many boobs hanging out in one place before. Older men had younger girls draped on their arm and older women with younger men pranced around, showing off their eye candy.

"Have I told you how gorgeous and stunning you look?" Nathan whispered as he leaned close to my ear.

"No, but thank you." I took a sip of my champagne.

"I'll be right back; there's someone I need to speak with."

Out of the corner of my eye, I saw someone familiar. I gasped as I took a closer look and saw it was John. He wasn't with the redhead I held a conversation with in the bathroom at the casino. He was with a tall leggy brunette, and actually, the redhead was much prettier.

"Fiona?" He cocked his head as he approached me.

"Hello, John."

"What are you doing here?"

"I was invited. What are you doing here?"

"Roger asked me to attend with him and his wife. There are a lot of business connections here. Hey, I'm sorry about your father. I heard you've taken over Winslow Wines."

"Thanks and I sure have. Living the dream." I help up my glass.

The leggy brunette walked over to where we were standing and placed her arm around him.

"Baby, who's this?" She shot me a look.

"This is Fiona. Fiona, this is Miranda."

"Nice to meet you, Miranda." I held out my hand.

"Likewise. How do you two know each other?" she asked with curiosity.

I could see the panic on John's ugly face as he fumbled with telling her that I was his ex.

"John and I went out a couple of times."

"So you're an ex-girlfriend?"

"No. I wouldn't call her that," he spoke.

Narrowing my eyes, I stared into his lying ones. If he wanted to play, then it was game on.

"No. I'm not an ex-girlfriend. We just had dinner a couple of times. It was purely business."

"Yes. See, Fiona is the CEO of Winslow Wines."

"Ah, okay." She smiled.

"Well, it was nice to see you again, Fiona. Take care," John spoke with a smug look across his face as he placed his hand on Miranda's back and led her away.

"Who was that?" Nathan asked as he walked up to me.

"That was John."

"As in your ex whose car you smashed up John?"

"Yes." I smiled. "Do you by any chance have a laptop on this fancy yacht of yours?"

"In my office. Why?"

"Can I use it for a minute, please?"

"What are you up to?" His eyes narrowed at me.

"I just have to check something."

"Follow me." He placed his hand on the small of my back as we made our way through the crowd and down to his office.

Sitting behind his desk, I hacked into John's cell phone.

"Fiona, seriously?"

I waved my hand as to shush him up and I went through John's text messages.

"Sorry, baby, but I have to cancel dinner tonight. Roger asked me to attend this cocktail party with him and his wife for work. I'll make it up to you, I promise."

"Aw, John, I was looking forward to seeing you."

"I know, baby. I'm so sorry. We'll get together tomorrow."

"Okay. I love you so much."

"I love you too, baby. Just hearing you say you love me is making me hard. I can't wait to fuck you in that beautiful sweet perfect ass of yours."

Ugh. Really? Did my eyes just really read that?

"Huh, he's quite the talker," Nathan spoke. "Did you ever let him do that?" He grinned.

"Wouldn't you like to know." I sneered.

I felt sorry for the redhead. She was clueless about the lying cheating scumbag she was dating. Just like I was. I started typing a message.

"Fiona Winslow!" Nathan exclaimed. "What are you doing?"

"You'll see." I smiled.

"Hey, baby, I miss you so much. Why don't you meet me at the party? I'm at the Marina Venice Yacht Club on a yacht. You can't miss it. Just get here as soon as you can. I'm dying to see that beautiful face of yours."

"What's the name of your yacht?" I asked.

"The Entertainer."

I rolled my eyes.

"The yacht is called the Entertainer." I typed.

"And what are you going to do when she responds to his text message and he sees it?" Nathan asked.

"He won't see it because it'll come to my phone." I smirked.

And just as I said that, my phone dinged.

"Oh my God. Really? I'm so excited. I'll be there as soon as I can. I love you."

"I love you too, baby. Hurry up."

Closing out of his account, I shut the top to Nathan's computer.

"You're going to break that poor girl's heart. You do realize that, right?"

"It's better she finds out now. I'm actually sparing her in the future."

"I have no words for what I just witnessed," he spoke as we walked out of his office and back to the party.

As Nathan was off talking with friends of his, I saw Miranda sitting on the bench by herself. Taking two glasses of champagne from the tray, I walked over and handed her one.

"Drink?" I asked with a smile.

"Sure. Thank you."

"Where's John?"

"He had to go to the bathroom."

"So, how long have the two of you been dating?"

"Four months."

I choked on my champagne as I took a sip. We'd only been broken up for two months, so he was seeing her, me, and the redhead at the same time.

"Are you okay?" Miranda asked as she placed her hand on my back.

"I'm fine. It just went down the wrong way. Four months. That's great. The two of you are a really cute couple." I choked out the words.

"Thanks. It was love at first sight for both of us. He swept me off my feet with the first words that ever came out of his mouth."

"And those words were?" I cocked my head.

"You have to be the most beautiful woman I have ever seen." She smiled.

My stomach churned and I felt the need to puke. I looked over and saw John approaching us with a panicked look on his face.

"Hello again, Fiona. What were the two of you talking about?"

"You." I smiled. "Miranda was just telling me how it was love at first sight. I'm really happy for you, John." I got up and placed my hand on his chest, wanting to rip his heart out right from his body.

"Thanks, Fiona. Can I talk to you for a moment? I have some business I want to go over with you."

"Sure."

He led me away from Miranda and over to a spot where there weren't many people.

"I'm really happy with Miranda, and I don't want you to screw things up," he spoke. "You broke up with me, remember? You broke up over text. Do you have any idea how bad that hurt me? I was devastated for weeks. And just when I thought I could never get over you, I found Miranda."

Holy shit! Was he for real? Who could just spew that kind of bullshit?

"Listen, John. I am really happy you found someone else. I was in a bad place and I just couldn't be committed to a relationship. I'm sorry I hurt you." The vomit started to rise in the back of my throat.

"Okay. I forgive you. Good luck with everything, Fiona." He smiled as he walked away.

I was gripping my glass so tight, it felt like it was going to shatter in my hand.

"May I ask once again what that was about?" Nathan walked over to me.

"He forgave me for breaking up with him over text. I had a nice little chat with his girlfriend and it seems they have been dating for four months."

"Huh?" Nathan cocked his head. "Wait a minute. He was seeing you, her, and the redhead all at the same time?"

"Yep." I finished off my champagne.

"Damn." He shook his head. "That guy sure has some balls. Are you okay?"

"I'm fine." I smiled. "You can thank him and my father for my mistrust of men." I walked away.

CHAPTER 24

Fiona

My phone began to ding with messages for John from the redhead.

"I'm here, baby."

Nathan looked at me and sighed. "Here we go."

"Go find a good spot to sit and watch the show." I smirked as I saw the redhead looking around for John.

I knew exactly where John was because my eyes never left him since I sent her that text message. I casually walked over to where the redhead was standing.

"Oh my gosh, hi!" I smiled as I placed my hand on her arm. "Do you remember me? We had a conversation in the bathroom at the casino a couple of months ago."

"Oh, yes! Hi. Wow, what a coincidence. How are you, sweetie?"

"I'm fabulous. A lot better than the last time we spoke."

"That's great. Listen, I'd love to stay and chat, but I need to find my boyfriend. He's waiting for me. Oh, I see him! We'll chat later, okay?"

"Okay." I smiled.

Making my way back to Nathan, I grabbed his hand and pulled

him with me a few feet from the railing where John was standing alone.

"Pretend we're talking."

"You worry me, Fiona. I won't lie."

"Oh, please, Mr. I-want-controlling-interest-of-your-company. He deserves it and you know it."

Nathan sighed.

The redhead walked up to John and gave him a big hug and kiss. The expression on his face was pure panic as he grabbed hold of her arm.

"What are you doing here?" he asked in a raging tone.

"What do you mean? You asked me to come."

"No I didn't! What the hell are you talking about? You need to leave right now!"

"But—"

I saw Miranda walking towards them.

"Oh shit." Nathan looked at me.

I raised my brow as I took the glass out of Nathan's hand and took a sip.

"John? What's going on here?" Miranda asked. "Who is she?"

"I'm his girlfriend," the redhead huffed.

"Excuse me? I'm his girlfriend."

John let go of the redhead's arm and threw his hands up in the air. The two women argued as John stood there in a pool of sweat.

"We've been together for eight months," the redhead raised her voice.

"And we've been together for four. What the hell is going on, John?" Miranda shouted.

John saw me staring at him and a look of rage crossed his face as I smiled at him and held up my glass.

"YOU! YOU DID THIS!" he shouted as he pointed at me and both women turned around.

"Looks like you've been busted." Nathan smirked.

"It appears so." I slyly smiled.

Walking over to John and the two women, I spoke, "This man you both love so much is a cheating, lying bastard. While he was dating me, he was dating you." I pointed to the redhead. "And while he was dating the both of us, he was also dating you." I pointed to Miranda. "Three women at once, John? Are you trying to make up for your incredibly small penis or something?" I smirked.

"Why you fucking little bitch!" He lunged at me, I took a step back, and Nathan walked up.

"I suggest you back off right now before you end up in the hospital."

"Mr. Carter," he gulped.

"Fiona happens to be here with me tonight, so if you would like to settle this on the dock, I'd be more than happy to."

"She's with you?"

"Yes, and I know all about you and your little shenanigans."

"So you knew about them when we were together?" John glared at me.

"I knew of the redhead over here." I pointed. "I only found out about Miranda tonight."

"You. You were the one who fucked up my car." He shoved his finger in my face.

"I know nothing about that."

"You're a lying bitch," he shouted.

"Takes one to know one, darling."

"I'm calling the cops and having your ass thrown in jail for vandalism."

Nathan hooked his arm around him. "I wouldn't do that if I were you, John. Unless, of course, you never want to work in this city or any other city again. Are we clear?"

"Yes, Mr. Carter." He swallowed hard.

"Good. I'm glad you understand. Now, please leave my party and I never want to see you again."

John walked away with his tail between his legs and left both girls standing there crying.

"I'm sorry, ladies, but you needed to find out what kind of person he was before you became too invested in him." I walked away and headed off the boat.

"Where are you going?" Nathan asked.

"Home. I just need to go home."

He caught up with me and lightly grabbed my arm.

"I want you to stay."

"I can't. Please, Nathan, just let me go home."

"All right. Jason is down there. I'll have him drive you."

I gave him a small smile as I made my way to the dock and climbed into the back of the limo.

Nathan

I hated that she left. She was broken inside about so many things and all I wanted to do was fix her. I didn't condone what she did to John, but at the same time, I was turned on by her fearlessness. If only she'd show that with her business. I gave her a way out and she didn't want to accept it. I'd increase my investment to cover the money her father stole from the pension fund to save her and her company, but I wasn't changing the stipulation of taking over.

The party was coming to an end, so I had Jason drive me home and then I hopped into my Rolls Royce and headed to Fiona's, unannounced. Stepping onto her porch, I pulled my phone from my pocket and dialed her number.

"Hello."

"It's me. I'm standing on your porch."

I heard a long sigh and then she opened the door.

"Have you ever heard of calling someone before you come over to their house?" she spoke as she stood there looking sexy as hell in her short silk blue robe.

"I did call." I smirked.

"You were already here." She sighed.

"Are you up for some company?"

"You mean sex?" She arched her brow.

The corners of my mouth curved up into a smile.

"No. But I won't object if you want it."

"Come on in."

"I only came over to see how you were doing. You looked pretty upset when you left the party."

"That was very nice of you, but you could have just called."

"I could have, but I wanted to see with my own two eyes that you were okay."

"Aside from my life being a complete clusterfuck, I'm good."

"I can help you, Fiona." I placed my hands on her shoulders.

"I know you can, but with a price, and that price being the takeover my father's company."

"It's a business decision. It's nothing personal. I make sure I keep those two things very separate, and I suggest you learn to do the same."

"Give me a week," she spoke.

"A week for what?"

"To decide whether or not I'll accept your proposal."

"All right. You have a week and that's it. Any longer and I'm withdrawing the offer."

"You, Mr. Carter, are nothing but a corporate ass."

"I know." I grinned. "Now, you were saying something about sex."

She let out a light laugh and shook her head. Reaching down, I picked her up.

"That wasn't a no, was it?" I asked as I carried her up the stairs.

"What if it was?" She smirked.

"Too bad." My lips brushed against hers.

My hands tightly gripped her hips as she moved back and forth against my cock and a wave of warmth swept over me. Throwing my head back, I held her in place as I pushed every last drop of come I had in me inside her. She collapsed and I wrapped my arms around her, feeling her heart rapidly beat against my chest.

"That was incredible," she spoke breathlessly as she rolled off of me.

"That it was, beautiful. Shit. I still feel like I'm coming." I grinned as I looked over at her.

The happiness that was in her eyes a moment ago faded as she got up and slipped on her robe.

"What's wrong?" I asked.

"Nothing. I'm just thirsty. I'm going to head downstairs and get a glass of water."

Slipping back into my clothes, I went into the kitchen, where I found her standing over the sink with a glass in her hand.

"Be careful driving," she spoke without looking at me. "Do me a favor and send me a text so I know you made it home."

"I will." I walked over to her and kissed the back of her head.

Walking out of the kitchen and making my way to the front door, I stopped for a moment and clenched my fist. I didn't want to leave, but I couldn't stay. Taking in a deep breath, I opened the door and walked out, shutting it behind me.

CHAPTER 25

Fiona

I set my glass down and went upstairs. I sat on the edge of my bed, never having felt so alone. I wanted him to stay the night, in my bed, holding me in his strong arms. The way he stood up for me against John made me feel good, maybe even special. No one had ever done that for me before. He wouldn't have stayed anyway. It was something he didn't do with anyone. He was a relationship-phobe, and I wanted to know why. I had good reason as to why I didn't want to get involved with anyone. It was my mistrust of men. The feeling of being used, cheated on, and made to feel like I was nothing was too much for me to handle. I liked having sex with Nathan and no strings attached. The last thing I needed was to get involved in a relationship, give a part of my life to someone, and then have it come crashing down on me at any given moment. No thanks. I liked being on my own, doing things my way, and not have someone questioning me. But then, why did I feel so alone? I needed to talk to someone. A therapist, maybe. Someone who could shed some light as to why I was feeling this way. As I was pondering my thoughts, my phone dinged with a text message from Nathan.

"I'm home safe and sound. And look at that, you asked me to do something and I did. I didn't forget because I didn't want you to worry."

A smile crossed my face.

"Thank you. I appreciate it. I'm happy you're home safe."

"Good night, Fiona."

"Good night, Nathan."

I grabbed my travel mug, climbed into my car, and met Lydia at the Los Angeles Medical Center for her first OB appointment. While we were sitting in the waiting room, I told her everything that had happened last night.

"Damn, I wish I could have been there to see that."

"It was pretty funny. Especially when he came at me and Nathan stepped in."

The nurse called us back into the room and had Lydia lie down on the table while she prepped her for an ultrasound.

"Good morning, Lydia."

"Morning, Dr. Grant. This is my best friend, Fiona."

Holy shit on a cracker! Dr. Grant was the hottest doctor I'd ever seen. Tall, blue eyes, military-styled hair, and a light stubble that swept across his jaw.

"Nice to meet you, Fiona. Now, Lydia, let's see what's happening in that belly of yours. You said you took four pregnancy tests and they all came back positive?"

"Yes."

"Okay. We're going to start with an ultrasound and then we'll do some bloodwork."

I grabbed hold of Lydia's hand while Dr. Grant squeezed some gel on her belly and then slowly ran the wand across her.

"There's your baby." Dr. Grant smiled as he pointed to a small bean-looking thing on the screen. "And here's the heartbeat."

"Oh my God." Lydia looked at me with tears in her eyes. "That's my baby."

I won't lie and say tears didn't fill my eyes, because they did.

"Yeah." I smiled as I squeezed her hand.

"You are a little over eight weeks pregnant," Dr. Grant spoke. "I'm going to write you a script for some prenatal vitamins. You are to take them every day and I will see you in four weeks. Am I to assume the father won't be taking part in this pregnancy?"

"No. He won't."

"He's a Tinder scumbag," I spoke.

"Ah, yes, Tinder. I've been hearing a lot about that from my patients." He winked. "Have a good day, Lydia, and go get those prenatal vitamins. It was nice to meet you, Fiona."

"Thank you, Dr. Grant."

"Nice to meet you too." I sighed.

"Don't think I didn't notice you staring at him the whole time," Lydia spoke.

"You didn't tell me he was hot. Jesus, Lydia, how could you have him for a gynecologist?"

"I only saw him once when I switched birth control. His father was my gynecologist, but he retired three months ago and his son took over. I was just as shocked as you when he stepped in the room for my exam. I'm trying not to think about his looks. It's awkward."

"How can you not? Good lord."

We walked to the parking lot and hugged goodbye.

"Thanks for coming with me."

"Isn't that what best friends are for? And don't worry, I'll be coming to every appointment with you." I smiled.

"Down girl." She laughed.

"Morning, Josh," I spoke as I passed his desk and went into my office.

"Morning, Fiona. Three more vendors cancelled their contracts, bringing the total to over thirty stores that will no longer be selling Winslow Wines."

"Great." I rolled my eyes. "What else?"

"I got some info on each of the board members." He smiled.

"Good stuff?"

"Yeah. I'd say some really good stuff." He handed me the manila folder.

"I'll look through it later and hopefully I will never have to use it."

"Oh, Robbie wants to see you in his office."

I sighed. "Do you know what about? Because I really do not feel like dealing with him."

"I have no clue."

"Thanks, Josh."

I promised myself when I woke up this morning that today was going to be a great day. I was going to be positive and work my ass off to try and find a solution to Winslow Wine's financial issues. Getting up from my desk, I went into my Uncle Robbie's office.

"You wanted to see me?"

"Yes. Have a seat." He sighed. "Has Nathan Carter given you the proposal yet?"

"He has." I nodded.

"And?"

"I told him to give me a week to think about it."

"A week? Fiona, what the hell are you waiting for? We need him to invest now!"

"He wants controlling interest."

Leaning back in his chair, he interlaced his fingers. "Maybe that's the best thing for this company."

"Oh really? So you don't think I can run this company either?"

"I didn't say that, Fiona. So don't put words in my mouth. The timing of your father's death and the takeover of this company wasn't a good one and we're running out of time. If there's a way to save this company, we need to jump on it."

"And we will. I have a week to figure things out."

"I've been trying to figure things out for the past two years since that bad business deal your father made. How are you going to do it in a week?"

"Well, sitting here and talking to you is cutting into my time." I got up from my chair. "So, if you'll excuse me, I have some things to figure out."

As I lay my forehead down on my desk, I was interrupted by Josh.

"Taking a nap again?" he spoke.

"Go away. I need to think."

"Your stepmother is on line one for you."

"Really?" I lifted my head and looked at him.

"Yes, really." He smirked.

Taking in a deep breath, I picked up the phone.

"Hey, Rachel."

"Hi, Fiona. I was wondering if you'd like to come over tonight for a home cooked meal?" she spoke with a hint of sadness in her voice.

I hadn't seen her since after the funeral and, in a way, I kind of felt bad about it. She didn't have any kids and all of her family lived in Florida.

"Sure. What time?"

"Wonderful." Her voice perked up. "Is five o'clock good?"

"I'll see you then."

After hanging up with her, I lay my head back down on my desk, and once again, I was interrupted. But this time, it wasn't Josh's voice I heard.

"I see you're hard at work," Nathan spoke.

Lifting my head up, I couldn't help but smile at the sexiness that stood before me. All six feet of him.

"I'm thinking."

"Do you always think like that?" He took a seat across from my desk.

"Sometimes. Now what can I do for you, Mr. Carter?"

"Oh, I can think of a lot of things you can do for me." He smirked. "Especially a little something that happened in the shower the other morning."

"Shh! Do you want people to hear you?" I tightened my legs at the thought.

"Your door is shut. Nobody can hear us. Anyway, I was hoping that maybe you spent the day yesterday giving my proposal some more thought."

"You gave me a week, Nathan."

"I know. Maybe it was just an excuse to see you." The corners of his mouth curved up into a smile.

"You could have just called and asked me to dinner."

"I could have, but you probably would have turned me down."

"You're right, I would have. I'm having dinner with my stepmother tonight."

"See, then it's a good thing I dropped by."

I gave him a small smile as I looked down.

"I have to get going. I have a business meeting." He got up from his chair, walked over to me, kissed my forehead, and gave me a wink.

"Have a good day, Mr. Carter," I shouted as he opened the door.

He stopped and turned around. "I already am." He smiled.

CHAPTER 26

Fiona

Opening the door to my father's house, I could somehow still feel his presence. I hadn't been back here since the funeral. I told Rachel to call me when she was ready to pack up his things, but I hadn't heard from her, so I assumed she wasn't ready yet.

"Hi, Fiona." Rachel walked into the foyer and hugged me.

"How are you doing?" I asked.

"Just when I think the days will get easier, they don't. Dinner's ready. Come sit down."

"Rachel, did my father ever talk to you about the financial troubles Winslow Wines is having?"

"No. He never said a word. How bad is it?" she asked.

"Pretty bad. Actually, we're on the verge of bankruptcy."

"Oh no. I'm sorry." She placed her hand on mine. "I had no idea. But then again, your father very rarely talked about the business with me. He left the business at the office the minute he stepped through that door."

"Have you boxed up all his things yet?" I asked.

"No. I know I should, but I just can't yet."

"It's okay. Just let me know when you're ready and I'll help you."

After finishing dinner, I helped Rachel clean up and then stepped inside my father's home office. I hadn't been in here since before he passed away. Sitting down behind his mahogany desk, I ran my fingers along the roped edges and tears began to fill my eyes.

"What am I supposed to do, Dad? You left me with a mess and the only way out is to give someone else control of the company you built. I don't want to disappoint you again, but I have no other choice." A tear streamed down my cheek.

"Fiona?" Rachel softly spoke as she stepped inside.

Wiping the tear away, I got up and took in a deep breath.

"Sorry."

"Don't be," she spoke as she walked over to where I was standing and wrapped her arms around me. "I miss him every day."

"There's an investor who wants to invest in Winslow Wines but with the stipulation that he takes controlling interest in the company and I don't know what to do." I took a seat behind my father's desk.

"If the company is in that much trouble, it sounds like you don't have a choice," she spoke. "Listen, Fiona, you father didn't plan on dying when he did and he certainly didn't want you to take on the burdens he was facing. That wasn't his intention when he appointed you CEO. If you're worried about disappointing him, don't be. If this is the only way to save the company, then you need to do what's best for you and Winslow Wines. That's what your father would want."

"Maybe you're right. Thanks, Rachel." I gave her a small smile. "I should get going."

"Thanks for having dinner with me. Don't be a stranger, okay?" She grabbed hold of my hand.

"I won't."

As I was getting into my car, my phone rang and it was Lydia calling.

"Hello."

"Please tell me you still aren't at the office or at home in your pajamas."

I let out a light laugh. "No. I just left Rachel's house. We had dinner."

"Oh good. Please say you'll go with me to Palomino's? I'm dying for their Palomino burger and since you already ate, you can get those Sicilian donuts you love so much."

"Are you having a craving that bad?" I sighed.

"Yes, and I'd ask my boyfriend, but—oh wait, I don't have one."

Rolling my eyes, I agreed to meet her there.

"I'll call right now and reserve us a table," she spoke with excitement.

"Okay. I'll see you in about twenty minutes."

Stepping inside the restaurant, I told the hostess I was meeting Lydia and she immediately took me over to the booth where she was already sitting.

"Sorry. Traffic was a bitch from Rachel's house."

"It's okay. I already ordered my burger and your donuts." She smiled. "I'll be right back. I have to use the bathroom." She got up.

I sat there, sipping on my drink and looking around when I caught the back of a man's head sitting at a table across the restaurant. I'd swear it was Nathan. I knew that hair and corporate suit anywhere. He wasn't alone. Sitting across from him was a redhead. I had to be sure it was him before I let myself get all worked up. But how? I couldn't very well walk up to the table and make a fool of myself if it wasn't. Think. Think. Think. I sent a text message to my friend Lenny.

"*Lenny. I need to track where someone is.*"

"*Have I taught you nothing, Fiona? I'll send you the link to an app to download. If the person you're looking for has a cellphone on them, all you have to do is type in the number and the location of where this person is at will pop up on a map.*"

"*Thanks, Lenny. I owe you.*"

"*You're welcome, and no, you don't.*"

I downloaded the app and entered Nathan's number.

"What are you doing?" Lydia asked as she sat down.

"Tracking Nathan."

"Huh? Why?" she asked with a twisted face.

"Because I'm almost positive that man sitting over there across from the redhead is him."

"Where?" She whipped her head around.

The map opened up and, sure enough, he was here. That was him. I swallowed hard and my heart started to skip several beats.

"It is him."

"Oh," Lydia spoke.

Our waitress walked over and set our food down in front of us. Suddenly, I didn't want the donuts anymore. My belly felt sick and I just wanted to go home, but for Lydia, I didn't tell her that.

"So, like, you seem upset," Lydia said as she took a bite of her large burger.

"Who me? I'm not upset," I lied. "We aren't anything. We had sex a few times and that's it. So what if he kisses my forehead every time he sees me. So what that he took me to dinner in San Francisco. So what if he flew to Paso Robles just to see me. So what if he invited me to his party on his yacht and so what if we have sex every single time we're together!" I spoke through gritted teeth as I shoved a donut with chocolate sauce in my mouth.

"Yep. You're upset and I don't blame you. Go over there and tell him off."

"No. I can't. It isn't any of my business who he sees. Like I said, we aren't anything."

The fact that he was going to ask me to dinner until I told him that I was going to Rachel's and then asked another woman infuriated me. He quickly reminded me what a player and a womanizer he really was. And a redhead? Seriously? Fucker. How the hell was I supposed to tell him that I was accepting his proposal for Winslow Wines? He was the last man on earth I'd want to get into business with. But I had no choice. It was either swallow my pride or close the doors forever, leaving people out of work and with no pension. Not to mention that an investigation could be launched.

Nathan and the redhead got up from their chairs and began to walk our way.

"Shit! He's coming this way." I quickly got under the table so he wouldn't see me.

This was ridiculous. Why was I behaving this way? So what if he saw me? Then he'd have to come up with some quick excuse. Or maybe he wouldn't have an excuse and he wouldn't care if I saw them together. Either way, I was staying under the table until he was gone.

"They're gone." Lydia peeked under the table at me.

I let out a deep breath as I climbed out and back into my seat.

"Is everything okay?" the waitress asked as she walked by and saw me.

"Yeah. I dropped my contact." I casually smiled. "I'm accepting his proposal." I looked at Lydia.

"What? Why?"

"I have no choice. It's either that or shut down the company and go to jail for what my father did."

"Oh, Fiona. I'm sorry." She pouted.

"It's fine. From here on out, there will be no more Nathan Carter in my personal life. Only in my business life and I intend to keep the two very separate."

"I think in order to do that, you need therapy."

Shoving another donut in my mouth, I spoke, "I know. Do you know anyone?"

CHAPTER 27

*N*athan

After dropping Kylie off, I headed home and straight into my office to do some work. I poured a scotch and took a seat behind my desk, trying to concentrate on the contracts that needed to be looked over. But the only thing I could think about was Fiona. As I was in deep thought, my phone dinged with a text message from her.

"We need to meet tomorrow morning concerning the proposal."

"Okay. You've made your decision already?"

"Yes. When can you meet?"

I looked at my schedule for tomorrow and I was pretty much open all morning.

"How about nine o'clock? Unless you would like to meet now?"

"Nine is fine and no."

I frowned because I sensed an attitude coming from her.

"Then I'll see you tomorrow morning. I hope you enjoyed your dinner with your stepmother."

I waited and no response came from her. What the hell was her problem? I sighed as I got up from my desk, grabbed my keys, and headed over to her place. I wasn't standing for any attitude from her, plus, I wanted her and I wasn't taking no for an answer. If she was mad at me about something, there would be no way she'd answer the door, so I had to devise a plan. I looked at my watch and noted that the florist was still open.

"May I help you, sir?" the older woman behind the counter asked.

"I need the biggest floral arrangement you have."

"Okay. Follow me to the cooler and I'll show you a couple."

Following her, I picked out one with a mixture of all different kinds of exotic flowers.

"Is your delivery person still here?"

"We're just getting ready to close, so I'm sorry, they can't be delivered tonight."

"It's not an option." I pulled out my wallet and handed her a hundred-dollar bill. "I'm sure your delivery person would like to make a hundred dollars right now."

"Seriously?" She frowned.

"Yes. Seriously."

"Teddy," she yelled.

A moment later, a young man, who had to be at least six foot four, came from the back.

"This gentleman would like you to deliver these flowers. He's including a hundred-dollar tip."

"Sure thing." He smiled.

Walking with him to his delivery truck, I handed him Fiona's address.

"Thank you. I appreciate it." I smiled.

"No, thank you, sir."

We both arrived at Fiona's house at the same time. I stood to the side while he rang the doorbell.

"Who is it?" she asked.

"I have a flower delivery for a Miss Fiona Winslow."

I could hear the clicking of the locks and then the door opened.

"Oh my gosh, how beautiful and big."

"I can bring it inside for you," the delivery guy spoke.

"No thank you. I can take them."

Good girl.

"Let me help you." I smirked as I stepped from the side and in front of her door.

"Nathan, what the hell?"

I took the arrangement from her and walked inside, setting them down on the dining room table.

"Are those from you?"

"Yes."

"Why?"

"Because I sensed an attitude in your text messages and I didn't like it."

My cock was already on the rise just by standing there and staring at her in the satin robe she wore.

"So you had a delivery guy deliver the flowers for you even though you were coming over?"

"Yep. I sure did. I knew with your attitude, you probably wouldn't have answered the door if you knew it was me."

"Aren't you on a date or something?" she asked with an attitude as she walked past me.

"No. Why would you ask me that?"

"Never mind. Please just leave. I'm tired."

"No. I'm not leaving, Fiona. What did you mean by that?" I asked as I lightly took hold of her arm.

"I saw you tonight at Palomino with a redhead!" she yelled.

The corners of my mouth curved upwards as her jealousy turned me on. I pulled her into me without even offering an explanation, as my cock was now standing at full attention, and smashed my mouth against hers. At first, she tried to pull away but then stopped resisting as soon as my fingers traveled up her short silk robe, pushed her panties to the side, and dipped inside her. She gasped and so did I when I felt the wetness emerge from her.

"Do you want me to stop?" I whispered.

"No," she replied breathlessly.

With my fingers still inside her, I led her to a bare wall, which was perfect for me to fuck her. Untying her robe with my free hand, I slid if off her shoulders and let it drop behind her. She was wearing a short pink nightie that I found incredibly sexy. So sexy that I wanted to fuck her in it. Our lips met again as my hands roamed up and down her body, while hers tugged at my belt. Hooking my fingers around the sides of her panties, I took them down. Taking my shirt over my head, I threw it across the room as she successfully took my pants down, releasing my throbbing cock that couldn't wait to be inside her.

"You're so damn beautiful," I spoke in a low voice as I took her arms and held them above her head with one hand.

Our lips locked together as I thrust into her, making sure my cock was buried deep inside. Breaking our kiss, my tongue slid down the front of her neck and swept over her breasts, which were lightly covered by her nightie, leaving my imagination to run wild. She panted as I moved rapidly in and out of her. Letting go of her wrists, I placed both of my hands under her ass and held her firmly as she wrapped her beautiful long legs around my waist and I buried my face into the side of her neck.

She swelled around me and let out several moans as her legs tightened and she had an orgasm. There was no holding back as I thrust one last time, my moans heightened by the warmth that enveloped me. My cock exploded deep inside her. After our racing hearts calmed, I pulled out of her and gently set her down. Our eyes locked onto each other's and not a word was spoken. After pulling up my pants, I slipped my shirt back on, kissed her forehead, and headed towards the door.

"By the way, that woman you saw me with tonight, her name is Kylie and she's my assistant. It's her birthday today. I was supposed to take her to lunch, but I got held up in a meeting, so I took her to dinner instead. She used to be a brunette but decided to become a redhead as of yesterday. Next time, just ask me instead of getting an instant attitude." I winked. As I opened the door, I looked at her once again. "I thought you had dinner at your stepmother's house?"

"I did. I was having dessert with Lydia," she softly spoke.

"I hope you enjoyed it. Have a nice night, Miss Winslow, and I'll see you tomorrow morning." I smiled as I walked out the door.

CHAPTER 28

Fiona

I stood there, unable to move myself away from the wall, my body still tingling from him and my mind in a chaotic state of passion. His assistant? I bit down on my bottom lip with a small smile. Grabbing my robe and panties from the floor, I walked over to the beautiful flower arrangement he gave me and took in the different scents that radiated from them. I had a problem. I gave in to him before I knew he was with his assistant. I didn't mean to, but my body wasn't about to turn him away. It craved him, every inch of him. How long could this go on for? I was getting myself in deeper every day and soon it would be impossible to keep my personal life and business life separate. As long as he was around, there couldn't be a separation, and now, my life and my head were royally fucked.

The next morning, around eight o'clock, I stepped into my Uncle Robbie's office.

"Good morning, Fiona. What can I do for you?"

"I wanted to let you know that Nathan Carter will be here around nine o'clock for a meeting. I've decided to accept his business proposal."

"That's music to my ears, my darling niece." He smiled as he got up from his desk and hugged me.

"Yeah, well, I have no choice and you know it."

"I know and I'm sorry, but you're doing the right thing."

"I hope so."

Walking to my office, I asked Josh to follow me inside.

"What's up, boss?"

"I'm going to accept Nathan Carter's business proposal and I wanted you to hear it from me first."

"Are you sure you know what you're doing?" he asked.

"Semi-sure." I took a seat behind my desk. "Just send him in when he gets here."

"Will do."

I looked at the clock. It was eight fifty-nine. He had exactly one minute to get his tight, perfectly shaped ass into my office. The clock struck nine and he and Will came strolling in.

"Good morning." Nathan smiled.

"Good morning, gentlemen. Please have a seat." I got up from behind my desk.

Nathan's eyes raked over me from head to toe, making me uncomfortable but horny at the same time.

"I've decided to accept your business proposal, but there are stipulations I want in place."

"What stipulations?" Will asked.

"No one in my company is to be let go. No bringing in your people and no getting rid of mine."

"Done," Nathan spoke.

"Also, when we start turning a profit again, I want my company back. I will pay you back your investment plus a percentage of the profits."

Nathan leaned back in his chair and cocked his head.

"And you think you can do that so easily?"

"I know what I'm capable of with the right funds, and I have no doubt that Winslow Wines will be up and running again very soon."

He narrowed his eye at me as he sat there with a smirk on his face.

"If you can triple your profit within the first year of our deal, consider it done. If you can't, we're staying. I also have a request I would like fulfilled," he spoke.

"And what is that?" I cocked my head as I leaned back against my desk.

"I want an office here."

"Excuse me?"

"You heard me. At least a desk. Preferably right in that corner over there." He pointed.

"In my office?" I laughed.

"Yes. I won't be here much, but when I am, I'll need a place to sit and work. After all, I will own the company, so it's only natural I have a place to sit. Right?" His brow arched.

"Do you have a place to sit in all the other businesses you own, Mr. Carter?"

"No. But Winslow Wines is one I'm especially passionate about." He grinned.

My legs voluntarily tightened and I let out a sigh.

"Fine. You can have your desk since it will only be temporary." I smirked. "Have your attorneys draw up the final contract. We'll send it over to mine and then present it to the board. The sooner we can get this deal moving, the sooner we can get the company back on track."

"You've made the right decision, Miss Winslow." Nathan got up from his seat and held out his hand.

"It's a pleasure doing business with you." Will did the same.

"Will, if you'll excuse us for a moment, I need to speak with Nathan alone."

"Sure. I'll wait out in the hall."

"Still thinking about last night." Nathan smiled.

"No. Actually, I'm not. I just wanted to tell you that since we're going to be working together, we need to keep it on a professional basis only."

"Why?"

"Because anything else leads to complications and I don't want there to be any. My main focus is Winslow Wines and that's how it's going to stay."

"Okay, then. A professional basis only." He was all too eager to answer.

"Thank you." I nodded.

"Are we finished here?" he asked.

"Yes."

I walked him over to the door, and when we stepped outside my office, I saw Lydia talking to Will.

"Lydia, what are you doing here?"

"I need to talk to you." There was a sadness in her eyes, and suddenly, I started to panic.

"Come on in. Gentlemen, it was nice to see you." I gave a small smile, walked into my office, and shut the door.

"What's wrong? Is it the baby?" I asked.

"No. The baby is fine. I got let go today."

"WHAT?!" I exclaimed. "Why?"

"Bryce decided it was time to make some cuts. He made them in other departments as well. Since you left, clients have dropped. They said that if you couldn't handle their accounts, they were going somewhere else."

"I'm sorry." I hugged her.

"What am I going to do?" She began to cry. "I have a baby on the way and no job. How the hell am I supposed to support this kid?"

"You listen to me." I broke our embrace and clasped her shoulders. "What have you been talking about for the last couple of years?"

"What?" She looked at me in confusion.

"You want to start your own business. Now's the perfect opportunity. You have enough money saved to get by for a while. Start your own freelance business. You already do some work on the side. Turn it into full-time. Just think, no more getting up at the crack of dawn to go to work for that asshole. No one telling you what to do. You're your own boss, Lydia. When one door closes, another one opens."

"Are you going to take your own advice?" She smiled.

"I'm different. I'm a mess. You're not."

"Maybe you're right. Maybe this is a blessing."

"It is. Now go home and start planning out your business. If you need help, call me."

"Thank you." She hugged me. "I don't know what I'd do without you."

"Same." I pouted as I kissed her cheek.

"By the way, that Will guy, Nathan's friend, he's really hot and seems really nice. We were talking a bit while waiting for you and Nathan."

"Yeah. Don't." I shook my head.

She rolled her eyes. "I'm going home now. I'll call you later."

As soon as she left, I took a seat behind my desk. That asshole Bryce knew she was pregnant and needed that job, plus the insurance. She was one of the most talented graphic artists at that company, and for him to let her go was inexcusable.

CHAPTER 29

Nathan

"I can't believe you agreed to her stipulations," Will spoke in irritation as we climbed inside the limo.

"I know what I'm doing. Do you really think she can triple profits in the first year?"

"No."

"Neither do I. Anyway, she told me that our relationship needs to be strictly professional."

"Why? And what relationship? You have sex with her like every other woman. There's no relationship there."

I didn't say a word and stared out the passenger window.

"Are you upset she said that? I mean, you can still sleep with her and do business together. People do it all the time. Obviously, she thought there was a relationship thing there. Women are always thinking that. We fuck them and, bam, you're suddenly in a relationship."

I didn't respond to his remark.

"That friend of hers, Lydia, she's smoking hot and she seems nice. It's weird. I felt really comfortable with her even though we only spoke for a few minutes."

"She's pregnant." I looked over at him.

"Oh. So she's married?"

"No. The baby daddy isn't in the picture. Some Tinder guy that lied to her."

"That sucks. I was going to ask her out, but now that I know she's pregnant, forget it."

"Yeah. I wouldn't get involved with that if I were you."

After returning to the office, I found myself extremely irritated. Irritated by what Fiona said about keeping a professional relationship. I wasn't exactly sure what I wanted and it was probably best that I kept my distance from her for a while until I figured it out. I had become too wrapped up in her. Hell, I bought her flowers and I never bought the women I slept with flowers. I was confused and being in a Fiona-free zone for a few days was exactly what I needed. If she wanted a professional only type of thing, then that was what she'd get.

CHAPTER 30

Fiona

A few days had passed and I hadn't heard a word from Nathan. I spent my days at the office trying to smooth over the creditors and promising them they'd get their money. The contract between Winslow Wines and Carter Management Group was delivered by Nathan's assistant Kylie and I took them over to our attorney.

"Everything looks to be in order, Fiona. All you have to do is sign and it's a done deal," my attorney, Lex spoke.

"Thanks, Lex. I'll call an emergency board meeting and we'll get this settled."

I had Josh call the board members to meet tonight at seven o'clock.

"Do you want me to call Nathan?" he asked.

"No. I'll call him myself."

The truth was I missed hearing his voice. I had no clue why he hadn't been in contact with me or why he had his assistant bring over the contract. I tried not to think about him, but it was hard. I missed him, but I felt used. There was a part of me that felt like he slept with me and tried to see me so much because he wanted me to agree to his terms about the company. Once he got his way, he disregarded me as if nothing between us ever happened. I knew what I said to him about keeping our relationship professional, but I didn't mean for him to stop coming around. Was he mad? Or was his game over with?

After Josh went back to this desk, I took in a deep breath and dialed Nathan.

"Nathan Carter."

"Hi, Nathan. It's Fiona."

"Yes, I know. What can I do for you?"

His tone sounded cold and I didn't like it.

"I got the contract back from my attorney and there's a board meeting at seven o'clock. If all goes well, we can sign tonight."

"I'll be there. Is there anything else?"

"No. How have you been?"

"Good. Listen, Fiona, I'm in the middle of something. I'll see you later."

"Yeah. Okay."

***

I was sitting in my office, doing some work and waiting until the board meeting when I heard a light knock on my office door.

"Come in."

When I looked up, Nathan walked through the door. My belly flipped at the sight of him.

"Hi." I smiled.

"Are you ready for the meeting?" he asked with a serious tone.

"Yeah." I grabbed the contract and walked with him to the boardroom.

The board of directors welcomed Nathan with open arms and I was insulted. Picking up the pen that was lying on the table, Nathan signed first and then handed the pen to me. As soon as I signed my name on the dotted line, a tear formed in my eye. I didn't expect it to be so hard, but it was. I felt like I handed him my soul. After signing, I threw the pen down, walked out of the boardroom, grabbed my purse from my office, and ran the hell out of the building as fast as I could without saying a word to anyone. Climbing into my car, I took off out of the parking lot and headed home, where I curled up on the couch and wrapped myself in a blanket.

About an hour had passed and there was a knock on the door.

"Fiona, it's me. Open up." He pounded.

"Go away, Nathan."

"If you don't open the door, I'm going to keep pounding until the neighbors come out."

Taking in a deep breath, I got up from the couch and opened the door.

"What do you want?" I asked in anger.

"Why did you run out like that?"

"Because I was tired and I wanted to get home." I walked back to the couch.

"I don't believe you." He stood in front of me.

"Nathan, why are you here? I haven't heard from you in days. I signed the damn contract, come home, and now you want to know what's wrong? Fuck you!" I shouted.

"Is that why you're so upset? Because you haven't heard from me in a few days? Why would that upset you? You're the one who said you wanted to keep things between us professional."

"Well, considering you were going to take over my company, I would have expected to at least hear from you. For god sakes, you even had your assistant bring the contract to me."

"Because I was busy. You're not the only company I've invested in," he shouted.

"Don't you shout at me!"

"You shouted at me first and said fuck you!"

I got up from the couch and attempted to walk away until he grabbed hold of my arm.

"Don't walk away from me."

I was ready to go psycho on him, to unleash the inner beast that was trying to claw its way out. But instead, I took in a long deep breath because it wasn't worth it.

"I'm sorry for saying that to you. You need to understand how hard all of this is for me. I've lost my parents and now I've had to sign over the company that my father worked so hard to build. I know I didn't have a choice because he's the one who made the mess, but it's still hard."

His grip on my arm loosened and he pulled me into him, holding my head against his chest.

"I know it must be hard and I'm sorry. But you made the right decision."

Being wrapped up in his arms made me feel better and I hated myself for feeling that way. Nathan Carter wasn't good for me. He had just as many demons inside of him as I did.

"Do you feel better now?" he asked.

"A little bit." I broke our embrace. "How about a vodka on the rocks?"

"I'd love one."

I walked into the kitchen and took down two glasses.

"How's Lydia doing? She looked really upset that day I was at your office."

"That asshole, Bryce, let her go."

"Why?"

"Because of cutbacks. Apparently, since I left, they lost some pretty major accounts."

"Really?"

"Is that so hard to believe?" I asked with a small smile as I handed him a glass.

"No. Not at all. Does he know she's pregnant?"

"Yes. And now she's losing her insurance."

"What an asshole. What is she going to do?"

"She wants to start her own graphic design business. She's been doing some freelance work on the side for about a year."

"Maybe I could help out. Some of the companies I own could probably use a good graphics designer. I'll give them a call and see if I can throw some business her way."

"Thanks, Nathan. I'm sure she'd appreciate it."

He finished off his drink and set his glass down.

"I better get going. Are we good?" he asked.

"Yeah. We're good." I smiled.

"I handed a check over to Robbie and he's going to deposit it tomorrow morning. The first thing we need to do is pay off the vineyard so they can start shipping the grapes to the winery and put the money back into the employee pension fund. Then we'll work on the rest of the creditors."

"I want to find a new vineyard. Start fresh, maybe make some changes. The same wine has been around for twenty-five years and times have changed; tastes have changed. Consumers have changed and I think it's time for Winslow Wines to make a change."

"That's fine, but we need to start production back up as soon as possible so we'll use who we have for now until we find someone new."

"I agree."

He gave me a small smile as he walked towards the door. Before stepping outside onto the porch, he turned and looked at me.

"I'm happy that you're feeling better about things. Enjoy the rest of your evening."

"Thanks. You too, Nathan."

As soon as he shut the door, I locked up and went upstairs to my bedroom. My feelings for him were growing stronger every day and I didn't know how to stop them. He couldn't commit himself to anyone, that much was obvious by his statements. My reaction to him having dinner with his assistant, before I even knew who she was, frightened me. Jealousy reared its ugly head and coursed through my veins. That was why a personal relationship with him had to stop. I couldn't live like that, knowing how he was with women. All I wanted was to be a person's someone special. But with my trust issues, I wasn't sure that I could ever be.

CHAPTER 31

*F*iona　　I was sitting in my office when Uncle Robbie walked in.

"Good news, Fiona. The money has been put back in the pension fund and I've spoken to Ken Raines. He was pleased that our debt was paid and he said he'd start shipping out the grapes to the winery as soon as tomorrow, but he wants payment up front from now on."

"Why?"

"I'm not sure. I don't think he trusts us."

"Well, that's not how we do business. He ships, we pay later."

"You need to understand where he's coming from. We were in debt with him for over two million dollars for a long time. It's going to take a while for him to trust this company again. Now, if you'll excuse me, I have some other creditors to pay off. You did the right thing, Fiona. I can already see this company starting to turn around."

I gave him a small smile as he walked out of my office. My phone rang and when I looked at it, I saw that Lydia was calling.

"Hi there."

"You are never going to believe who I just got off the phone with."

"Who?"

"That friend of Nathan's. Will."

"What did he want?"

"He wants to have lunch to look over some of my designs. He may have some freelance work for me. Did you say something to Nathan?"

"Yeah. He saw you were upset that day you were here and he asked about it. I told him how you got laid off and he said maybe he could help."

"Wow. Thank you, Fiona. I love you so much."

"I love you too and you're welcome. I know everything's going to work out."

"I hope so. I'll let you get back to work. I have to go find something cute to wear." She laughed.

"Have a good lunch and let me know how it went."

"I will."

After ending the call, two men walked into my office and grabbed the couch that was sitting in the corner.

"Excuse me." I got up from my chair. "What do you think you're doing?"

"Moving this out of here. We have a desk that needs to be brought in."

Ugh. Nathan.

"You knew I was moving a desk in here," Nathan spoke as he walked in.

"I didn't think it would be today or this week, or even this month." I smirked.

"The sooner the better." He smiled. "How are you today, Miss Winslow?"

"So are we moving this out or what?" the big burly man with the stained t-shirt asked.

"Yes. Move it out of here," Nathan spoke.

Taking a seat behind my desk, I spoke, "I'm fine, Mr. Carter, and you?"

"I'm great."

The two men moved out the couch and brought in a glass-topped desk to put in its place.

"Move it out more," Nathan spoke. "The chair will be going against the wall."

"Your chair can go on the other side," I spoke.

"It could, but the view is much better with the chair against the wall." He smirked.

Damn him! I tightened my legs.

As soon as the men moved the desk forward and brought in a high back, dark brown leather executive chair, Nathan took a seat and smiled as he looked at me.

"Yes, the view is much better."

"Don't you have work to do?" I asked.

"Yes, but I wanted to make sure my desk was put in place first." He got up from his chair. "Anyway, I have to go out of town for a few days on business."

"Where are you going?"

"Does it matter? It doesn't have anything to do with Winslow Wines."

"No. It doesn't matter."

"Good. I have to go. My plane will be leaving soon. Try to stay out of trouble while I'm gone." He winked.

"I will, and I suggest you do the same."

"I can't make any promises." He smirked as he walked out of the office.

I clenched my fists, and after letting out the deep breath I took in, I grabbed my phone.

"Fiona, darling. It's been forever," Carlos answered.

"Hello, Carlos. I need a huge favor. Like huge."

"Anything for you, darling."

"How soon can you come to my office at Winslow Wines?"

"I can be there in a flash. What do you need?"

"We'll discuss it when you get here." I smiled.

"I'll see you soon."

I had just returned from the bathroom when I saw Carlos standing inside my office.

"Good to see you again, Carlos." I hugged him.

"Good to see you, Fiona. Now what's going on?"

"Look around. What do you see?" I waved my hand.

"Drab. Boring. Uninviting. But I do see potential."

"Excellent." I smiled. "I need to be inspired to do my best every time I sit behind my desk. I want people to feel welcomed, relaxed, and at home when they enter my office. I want it to scream California style."

"We can draw inspiration from the ocean." He held his hands out to his sides. "I see velvety saturated colored walls in dark teal, a wavy print floor-to-ceiling drapery on each of the windows, area rugs to match under each of the desks. Oh!" he exclaimed. "And cascading crystal strands hanging on the wall. Perhaps a couple of crystal lamps to match and teal-colored wingback chairs for your visitors."

"Perfect." I smiled. "I need it done and completely finished within a few days. I'm on a strict time schedule."

"Hmm." He looked down. "This carpeting needs to go. I'm thinking teal and white tiles in a checkerboard pattern."

"Sounds nice. Can you get it done within a few days?"

"Yes. Not a problem. We aren't starting a new job until the beginning of next week. I'll call my team now and have them come paint tonight. I hate to say this, Fiona, but you need a new desk. This one won't match the décor."

"Do what you have to do, Carlos. Out with the old and in with the new."

"I'll be in touch, darling." He kissed my cheek.

I went down to the storage area and collected some boxes so I could empty out the contents from my father's desk.

"Are you moving out?" Josh asked as I walked past his desk.

"I'm revamping my office."

"Nice. Is that what that guy was doing here?"

"Yes. My office will be under construction for the next few days, so

I'm going to be using the desk next to yours. We can be desk buddies." I smirked.

"Lovely." Josh rolled his eyes.

"I need you to call the movers and have them move all the furniture out of the office within the next couple of hours. Have them put everything in storage."

"Does Nathan know about this little revamp of your shared office?"

"No. He'll be so surprised when he gets back from his business trip. I can't wait to see the expression on his face."

Josh narrowed his eyes at me. "What are you up to, Fiona?"

CHAPTER 32

Fiona

After a long day of phone conferences with vendors, trying to coax them back to Winslow Wines, I went home and climbed into a hot, relaxing bubble-filled tub. It bothered me that Nathan wouldn't tell me where he was going. There was no reason for him not to tell me, unless he was hiding something. We would just see where Mr. Carter was at. I smiled as I took my phone and opened the tracking app. He was in New York, currently at the Plaza Hotel. I wondered if he was with someone or if he was alone.

Nathan

It was eleven o'clock here in New York and I should have been out at the strip clubs with some friends of mine, but I didn't feel like it, which was highly unusual for me. I had no interest in watching naked girls dance on the poles and give me cock-raising lap dances. What the fuck was wrong with me? I could tell you what was wrong. Fiona Winslow. She was the only woman whom I wanted to see naked and giving me a lap dance. I kept thinking about how jealous she was when she saw me at the restaurant with Kylie. The only reason women got jealous like that was when they were attracted to someone. I knew damn well if I saw her with another guy out somewhere, fists would be flying before I even knew who the person was. The thought of her with another man made my blood boil. It made me angry to even think about it. But I couldn't commit to her. It was just something I couldn't do. Committing to one woman was never in my life plan. I was happy with the way I lived my life. No one to answer to, no one to explain things to, no one nagging me about where I'd been or what I was doing. No one expecting things from me. Things I could never give. I liked being in control and controlling the women whom I took out and fucked. But Fiona Winslow was slowly taking all that away from me. She was uncontrollable. These few days away from her was what I needed.

Fiona

The last few days were hard without hearing from Nathan. Stepping inside my office, I gasped at the beautiful job Carlos did.

"Oh my God, Carlos, it's beautiful."

"Thank you, darling. I knew you'd love it."

"WOW!" Josh exclaimed as he walked in. "Fiona, it's amazing. Nathan is going to be so pissed." He laughed.

"He'll only be here sometimes, so he shouldn't have a problem with it."

I already knew that Nathan wasn't going to be happy. It was what he deserved since he moved a desk into my office just to taunt me.

"When's he coming back?" Josh asked.

"Let me check." I pulled out my phone. "He's already on his way back." I smiled as I held my phone up to him.

He shook his head and sighed. "Does he know you're tracking him?"

"Do you think he knows?" I raised my brow.

"Well, I'm going to get my phone ready for when he comes in here. I want to capture the reaction on his face when he sees what you've done."

I thanked Carlos and kissed him goodbye. Taking a seat behind my new rectangular glass-topped desk, I smiled. It was perfect and it made me happy. Okay, was I happy about the office or the fact that Nathan was going to be so pissed off? I had to admit it was a combination of both. He thought he was in control, but he was wrong. Dead wrong.

"Oh, Fiona." Carlos walked back in. "I almost forgot to give you this." He handed me a key. "The guys who ripped up the carpet found it taped down to the floor in the corner by the window."

"That's weird." I stared at it.

A few hours had passed and I was on my computer sending out some emails when I heard Nathan's voice.

"WHAT THE FUCK IS THIS?!"

Looking up at him, I smiled. "Welcome back."

"What the hell did you do, Fiona?" He stepped inside and Josh followed him, holding up his phone. "JOSH, OUT!" He shut the door and stood there glaring at me with a scowl on his face.

"What? I redecorated the office. Don't you like it? It needed a makeover. I wanted people to feel welcomed when they stepped inside. Don't you feel welcomed, Nathan?" I cocked my head.

He shook his finger at me. "Redecorating is one thing. Beige walls, blinds, carpet. Not this blue color."

"It's teal."

"I don't care what it is! And what's this?" He pointed to the crystal beads that hung from the wall. "Jesus, Fiona. I can't believe you did this. You did it on purpose." He continued to point his finger at me. "This is payback for me moving a desk in here."

"Don't be silly." I laughed. "It needed a makeover. It represents a new beginning here at Winslow Wines. Out with the old and in with the new. Plus, I agreed to you having a desk in here, remember?"

"You reluctantly agreed."

"You need to stop getting your panties in a bunch over this, Mr. Carter."

"Excuse me? Did I just hear you correctly?"

I threw my hands up in the air. "I don't know why you're so upset. This is MY office. Have you forgotten that?"

"An office in which I'll be spending some time. An office in which I have to sit in surrounded by blue everywhere I look."

"Teal."

He pursed his lips together and inhaled deeply through his nose.

"At least you still have a nice view from your desk, right?" I smirked.

In a calm tone, he spoke, "I'm leaving now." He walked to the door.

"Aren't you going to tell me how your trip was?" I asked.

"No." He scowled as he left.

CHAPTER 33

Nathan

I walked out of her office shaking my head but with a smile on my face. She wanted that kind of reaction out of me, so I gave her what she wanted. If she wasn't expecting it, she would have mentioned that she wanted to redo the office, but instead, she had it done, rather quickly, may I add, while I was away. I'd let her bask in her glory of thinking she royally pissed me off for a couple of days.

When I returned to the office, Will followed me in and took a seat across from my desk.

"I think I have a problem," he spoke.

"What's wrong?" I sat down.

"You know Fiona's friend, Lydia, the pregnant one?"

"Yeah." I arched my brow.

"I think I really like her."

"Like her how?" I narrowed my eye.

"I like spending time with her. We met for lunch the other day so I could look over her portfolio and get her some freelance work with a few companies and we ended up spending the rest of the day and most of the evening together, just talking. I haven't been able to stop thinking about her since. She's so easy to talk to and I feel like I've known her my entire life."

"She's pregnant, Will."

"I know." He sighed. "But I want to take her out. Like on a date. I called her last night about some bullshit excuse just to talk to her."

"She's pregnant, Will," I spoke again as I stared him in the eyes.

"Will you stop saying that? I know she's pregnant. I can't help that and I can't help that I want to see her again. Just like you with Fiona."

"Fiona's not pregnant, and if she was, I wouldn't be seeing her, and most importantly, I wouldn't be fucking her."

He got up from his chair. "Well, I can't think about her being pregnant right now. I want to get to know her better and I want to spend some more time with her. Maybe it's time we grew up, Nathan. We're thirty years old. You told me that you told Fiona about your mother and you have never spoke of that to anyone but me. What does that tell you?"

I sighed as I leaned back in my chair.

"Now if you'll excuse me, I'm going to call Lydia and ask her if she has plans for tonight. Maybe you and Fiona would like to join us."

"Fiona thinks I'm pissed at her."

"Why?" He frowned.

"She redecorated the office while I was gone. All girly-like with the color teal, crystal beads hanging from the walls, and fancy curtains on the windows."

He let out a roaring laugh. "Sounds like she did it on purpose to teach you a lesson about moving a desk for yourself in there."

"Yep. So I played it off as I was pissed and walked out."

"The two of you are quite entertaining." He shook his head as he left my office.

*J*ust as Jason pulled in, I saw Fiona sitting in her car in my driveway.

"Hello." I walked over to her window as she rolled it down.

"Hi. I need to talk to you. That is, if your panties aren't still in a bunch over the redecorating of the office."

I opened the door for her. "Stop saying that. Regardless of how mad I am, you need to talk to me, and being your business partner, I have to listen."

As soon as she climbed out, I shut the car door, walked to the house, and stepped inside.

"What's going on? Is this personal or business?" I arched my brow.

"Business."

"Wine? Or am I going to need something stronger?" I smirked.

"Wine is fine." She followed me into the kitchen and took a seat at the island.

"So what's going on?" I grabbed two wine glasses and a bottle from the wine cellar off the kitchen.

"When the guys were ripping up the carpet in the office, they found this taped to the floor in the corner." She held up a key.

"What's it to?"

"I have no idea."

Taking it from her hand, I examined it.

"This is a safety deposit box key."

"I know, and I went to the bank where we do all of our banking and it's not one of theirs."

"Then where is it to?" I asked as I pushed her glass towards her.

"I don't know. That's what I need to find out. There are hundreds of banks in Los Angeles. What I don't understand is why he felt the need to hide it under the carpet."

"Obviously there's something in that box he was keeping a secret and wanted to make sure nobody found that key. I'll tell you what, since tomorrow is Friday, I'll meet you at the office first thing in the morning and we'll start bank hunting."

"Thanks, Nathan. I appreciate it." She gave me a small smile. "I better get going."

I wanted nothing more than to hold her and kiss those beautiful lips of hers.

"I haven't eaten dinner yet. Have you?" I asked with the hope that she'd stay a while longer. I didn't want her to leave.

※

Fiona

I hadn't eaten dinner, but I couldn't tell him that. If I did, he'd want me to stay, and if I stayed, we'd have sex. My lower half was burning with desire for him. An ache so bad that it was unbearable. But I had to stay strong because we needed to maintain a professional business relationship. Eventually, sometime in the future, I wanted a relationship, marriage, and possibly a family. Nathan didn't want that, and as much as I had already fallen for his corporate ass, I needed to set myself straight because he wasn't a man that could love one woman. I wasn't even sure if he could love anyone enough at all.

"I did. I grabbed a bite to eat before I came over."

"Oh. Okay. I just thought I'd ask since you were here."

"I should get going." I pointed to the door in the awkwardness of the moment.

"Yeah. Probably a good idea." He placed his hands in his pockets.

"I'll see you tomorrow at the office."

"Yep. See you tomorrow, Fiona." He walked me to the door. "Oh, by the way, have you talked to Lydia?"

"Yeah. Why?"

"Did she mention anything to you about Will?"

"Why?" I narrowed my eye at him.

"Just curious. He really seems to like her. I was just wondering if she said anything about him."

"Just between me and you, she likes him as well. But I'm worried."

"Why?" he asked.

"Because I don't want her to get hurt. She's been through the ringer with guys and now she has a baby she needs to focus on."

"I'm not sure you have to worry about Will. He seemed pretty adamant about getting to know her better. As for getting hurt, that's something no man can promise."

I felt a stab in my heart when he said that. The look of seriousness in his eyes when he spoke those words confirmed for me that I was right about him all along. Being hurt by him was inevitable and it was something I was going to avoid at all costs.

"I guess." I gave a small smile. "Have a good night."

"You too, Fiona. Be careful driving home."

CHAPTER 34

Fiona

"Good morning, Josh," I spoke as I passed by his desk.

"Wait, Fiona!" He jumped up from his chair. "Don't go in there yet."

I stopped with my hand on the door handle, turned around, and glared at him.

"Why?"

"Well. Umm."

"Oh, for god sakes, Josh. I don't have time for his. Nathan is meeting me here and we're leaving." I opened the door, stepped inside, and gasped when I saw what was hanging on the wall over to the side of Nathan's desk.

"What the hell is that!" I yelled.

Josh came running in.

"I tried to warn you."

Hanging on the wall was a portrait of a woman sprawled out on a Victorian style-couch, in sheer lingerie, high heels, holding a glass of wine. I clenched my fists as I stared at the portrait and the only thing I saw was her long, red flowy hair.

"Where is he?!" I yelled.

"You wouldn't be asking for me in that tone. Would you?" I heard Nathan speak from behind.

"What's that?" I pointed to the portrait in anger.

The corners of his mouth curved upwards. "Isn't is beautiful?"

"Beautiful? It's trashy and doesn't belong here." I scowled as he took a seat behind his desk.

"It's not trashy at all. She's a beautiful woman holding a glass of wine. I found it fitting for the office." He smirked.

"In her underwear!"

"Tasteful lingerie, Fiona."

"I want it out!" I spoke through gritted teeth.

"I'm afraid I can't do that."

"And why not?" I placed my hands on my hips.

"Because I like it and it's my office too." He smirked.

"I'm the one who's here ninety-nine percent of the time and I'll be damned if I'm looking at that redhead all fucking day!" I yelled.

"Come on, Fiona. Stop getting your panties in a bunch over this. I think it looks great in here. You redid the office and I'm just adding my personal touch. It's no big deal."

I needed to calm down. I started it and he finished it. Taking in a deep breath, I threw my hands up in the air.

"Okay. You're right. Now let's go. God knows how long this is going to take."

We spent the next three hours traveling from bank to bank with no luck. I barely spoke a word to Nathan because I was still pissed off about the portrait he proudly hung in my office. We reached ProAmerica Bank and I was getting real tired of this.

"How can I help you?" the very pretty young blonde teller asked as she batted her eyes at Nathan.

"We were hoping you could tell us if this key belongs to your bank's safety deposit boxes." He flashed his sexy smile at her.

She took it from his hand and examined it. "No. This is a safety deposit box key from Bangor Savings Bank in Maine."

"How do you know?" I asked.

"I used to work there before I moved here to L.A. Their keys are cut differently than the standard safety deposit box keys and they have a B engraved at the very end of the key. See?" She pointed.

"Thank you." Nathan's grin widened.

"Yes, thank you." I nodded my head and got him the hell out of there as fast as I could before the young girl had an orgasm.

"What's he hiding in Maine?" I asked as we stepped outside the bank.

"I don't know. You haven't run across anything at the office pertaining to Maine?"

"No." I paced up and down the sidewalk.

"Fiona, get in the car," Nathan spoke.

"Hold on a second." I pulled out my phone and dialed Uncle Robbie.

"Fiona, where are you?" he answered.

"Out. I have a question. Has my father ever said anything to you about Maine?"

"The state?"

"Yes, Uncle Robbie, the state."

"No. He never said a word. Why?"

"I ran across something. I'll explain later. I'm going to be out of the office for the rest of the day."

"What's going on?"

"I'm not sure yet, but I'll let you know as soon as I find out."

After ending the call, I climbed into the back of the limo and Nathan slid in next to me.

"We have to go to Maine." I looked at him.

"I already called my pilot. We'll swing by my house first so I can pack a bag and then we'll stop at yours since it's on the way to the airport."

After stopping at both our houses, we drove to the airport and boarded Nathan's plane.

"I need a drink," I spoke as I sat in the big comfy leather seat.

"Wine or something stronger?" he asked.

"Something much stronger."

"Scotch?"

"Sounds good to me. How long is this flight?" I asked.

"The pilot said about five hours," he replied as he handed me my scotch and sat down in the seat next to mine.

"It'll be evening and the bank will already be closed."

"I know, so we'll go there first thing tomorrow morning."

Just before we took off, my phone rang and it was Lydia.

"Hello."

"You're going to Maine and don't bother telling me?"

"Sorry, Lydia. It was a last-minute trip. My dad has a safety deposit box at one of the banks in Bangor. Nathan and I are going to find out what's in it."

"Oh. Good luck. Anyway, I just wanted to tell you that Will and I had sex last night and it was amazing. And before you say anything, I was horny."

I sighed. "Okay. I won't say a word, at least not until I get back home."

"Have fun in Maine. I have to go get ready. Will's taking me to a movie tonight. Love you."

"Love you too."

"Did I hear her say that her and Will had sex last night?"

"Yes." I shook my head and stared out the window as we took off. "She said they're going to the movies."

"That's nice," Nathan replied.

"Yeah. It is." I stared out the window as I sipped on my drink.

"Would you like to watch a movie?" he asked.

Turning my head and looking at him, I smiled. "You have movies on this plane?"

"Of course. Just turn on the TV and pick one. You'll be more comfortable on the couch. I'm going to sit at the table over there and do some work."

"Okay."

Getting up from my seat, I walked over to the couch, sat down, and scrolled through the movies on the TV. I thought maybe when he asked me if I wanted to watch a movie, he'd watch it with me. To be honest, I was a bit disappointed. I ended up watching *Titanic* and I caught Nathan looking up from his laptop every now and again to see what was going on. By the end of the movie, I was a crying mess, especially when the credits began to play and Celine Dion's song "My Heart Will Go On" started playing. Nathan walked over, handed me a couple of tissues, sat down next to me, and pulled me into him.

"Why? Why did he have to die?" I sniffled.

"Because the movie directors are assholes."

I couldn't help but laugh as I pulled away from him.

"Sorry. You didn't have to come over here. I'm fine. I've only seen this movie a million times."

"It's okay. I'm done with work now anyway and you looked like you needed comforting." He smiled.

"Thanks." I dried my eyes.

"You're welcome. We better get back in our seats. We'll be landing soon."

After we landed and Nathan rented a car, we sat in the parking lot and I pulled up a list of hotels in the area.

"Oh, look at this hotel." I turned my iPad and showed him.

"Sorry, but that's a two-hour drive from here. You'll have to find another hotel."

"Aw, but this one looks so pretty." I pouted.

"I agree, but we're not driving two hours."

"Fine. There's a Residence Inn by Marriott only ten minutes away."

Once we arrived, we grabbed our bags and walked up to the lobby desk.

"How may I help you?" a polite young man asked.

"We need two rooms, please," Nathan spoke.

"You don't have a reservation?" he asked.

"No. We just flew in. It was an unexpected trip," I spoke.

Typing on his computer, he spoke, "I'm sorry, but we only have one room available and it's our studio with one king bed."

"How can you be fully booked?" I asked with irritation.

"I'm sorry, miss, but it is tourist season here in Maine. Just about every hotel is booked up. The only reason this one is available right now is because we had a cancellation this morning."

"We'll take it," Nathan spoke as he reached into his wallet and pulled out his credit card.

"How many nights will you be staying?"

"Just one," Nathan replied.

"You're all set. Here are your keys and you're in room 510."

"Thank you," Nathan spoke.

Now I was really irritated. Sharing a room with him all night was not on the agenda. *Shit. Shit. Shit.*

CHAPTER 35

Nathan

Sharing a room with Fiona was going to be extremely difficult. I had a hard enough time controlling myself around her as it was, and to be in the same room with her for an entire night might send me over the edge.

Opening the door, we stepped inside.

"Not bad," Fiona spoke as she walked over to the kitchen area and opened the refrigerator. "Yes! There's liquor in here." She smiled. "Oh, and they even have room service."

"Are you hungry?" I asked.

"Yes. I'm starving." She sat on the bed and looked over the menu. "And I'm tired and I want to take a shower."

"Then tell me what you want and you can take a shower."

"Can we get the cheese board?" she asked.

"You can get anything you want." I smiled.

"The cheese board, the lobster salad, and blueberry pie." She handed me the menu as she got up from the bed and went into the bathroom.

After placing the order, I changed into a pair of sweatpants and a t-shirt and sat on the bed with my back up against the headboard.

When the bathroom door opened, I looked up to see Fiona walking out in a pair of short pajamas, drying her hair with the towel.

"Don't say a word." She pointed at me. "This is awkward enough."

"Why is this awkward? We've had sex multiple times. I've seen every inch of you."

"But we aren't having sex anymore, you're my business partner, and our relationship is strictly professional."

"So. We still had sex." I smirked.

"Stop saying that." She walked back into the bathroom.

My cock was trying to get hard, but I had to quickly stop it when there was a knock at the door.

"Room service."

Getting up from the bed, I opened the door and a young man wheeled in a cart.

"Where would you like this set up?" he asked.

"This table over here is fine." I pointed.

After setting up our dinner, he left and Fiona walked over to the refrigerator and grabbed a bottle of Grey Goose from it and sat down.

"This looks delicious. What did you get?" she asked as she looked at my food.

"The roasted chicken BLT."

"Oh. That looks good too."

"Would you like a bite?" I asked as I held the sandwich up.

"No. I'm good with my salad."

For the first few moments, we ate in silence. There were so many things I wanted to say to her, but I couldn't.

"I'm sorry about the office," she spoke.

"About the redecorating?"

"Yeah."

"To be honest, I don't think it looks bad and I'm not mad. I know you did it on purpose."

"You're not mad?"

"No. I knew you wanted that reaction out of me, so I gave it to you." I smirked. "And to be fair, I'm sorry about the painting. I'll have it taken down when we get back."

"You did it on purpose to get back at me."

"Yeah. I did." I smirked as I took a bite of my sandwich.

"God, Nathan." She laughed. "How old are we?"

"I know, right? But I do want you to know that I have never acted like this before. You, Fiona Winslow, are teaching me your bad habits." I winked.

"Me? You're a supposed adult. You should know better. Me, on the other hand, I still have some growing up to do."

"I think I like you just the way you are." I smiled.

She looked down and didn't say a word. Maybe I shouldn't have said that, but it was something that just flew out of my mouth.

"Have you ever had a girlfriend?" she asked unexpectedly.

"No, and I'm not the romantic type either." I finished my sandwich.

"Why?" She cocked her head. "Seriously. Let's just be honest with each other."

"Why what? Why haven't I ever had a girlfriend or why am I not a romantic guy?"

"Both."

I shrugged and leaned back in my chair, draping one arm over the back.

"Relationships complicate a person's life. There are too many rules and expectations. Women expect things from a man that I just can't give."

"But if you love someone, those things are easy to give," she spoke as she took a bite of her blueberry pie.

"Love is overrated. People are taught to first follow their heart instead of their head, and to live happily ever after is just a myth. If you follow your heart first, you're setting yourself up for failure and disappointment in the future."

"Huh?" She cocked her head.

"Did you love John?" I asked. "Be honest, Fiona."

"No. I liked him, but I wasn't in love with him."

"Then why did you stay with him for a year?"

"I don't know. My mother had just passed away and I met him and he was nice. We got along, had stuff in common."

"So you followed your heart? You were upset because your mom had just passed away and he made you feel better, right? You were blinded by him because you needed someone to take away the pain. Now, if you would have listened to your head, you more than likely wouldn't have entered into a long-term relationship with him. Because I know somewhere in the back of your mind, you knew that jumping into a relationship so quickly while still mourning the death of your mother wasn't smart. But you let your heart take over. A heart that needed to be healed. Plus, didn't you tell me that you would have noticed he was cheating on you sooner, but you were too involved in trying to get that promotion at work?"

"Yes."

"See. You put your career in front of your relationship. You held that at a higher standard. That's what people do, Fiona. Nothing lasts forever. Something always becomes more important. That's why it's best just to go out, have some fun, and live life to the fullest. I don't believe you need love for that."

"Okay. And what about you not being a romantic guy?" she asked.

"If I'm romantic, won't that lead women on? Why do that to them when I have no plans on taking it any further than just sex?"

"I get what you're saying, Nathan, I really do. But I disagree with a lot of what you said."

"And that's fine. You don't have to agree. You asked and you wanted me to be honest with you, so I was. I think two people can be together and have a good time without the hassles of a relationship or commitment."

Who the hell was I trying to convince? Her or me?

"So really what you're saying is sex is all that's required with someone?"

"Well, not just sex. Companionship is nice too. Going to dinner, out for drinks, holding an intelligent conversation, and then sex." I smirked.

She sat there nodding her head as she pursed her lips.

CHAPTER 36

Fiona

I didn't know if growing up without a mother contributed to his attitude towards love and relationships, or if it was what he saw growing up with his father. Things were much clearer now that we had had this conversation. But then why couldn't I stop falling for him? What was the old saying? "You always want what you can't have?" I wanted him, but I knew I could never have him completely. Somehow, I didn't think that was going to stop me from wanting every inch of his sexy body now and again.

I got up from my chair, poured myself another vodka, and took it over to the bed.

"I'm going to finish this up and go to sleep. I'm exhausted."

"Okay." He walked over to the pullout sofa, took the cushions off, and attempted to pull the bed out. "What the fuck?"

"What's wrong?" I asked with a slight laugh as I watched him struggle with it.

"It's stuck. I can't get it out."

I had a dirty thought. It was the vodka that made me have it.

"That's so hot." I laughed.

He turned and looked at me with a smirk on his face.

"What's hot?"

"It's stuck and I can't get it out." I continued laughing. "Sounds very sexual."

"You have a dirty mind, Fiona. Now come over here and help me."

"Oh, big strong man needs help pulling out a sofa bed," I spoke in a low voice as I got up.

"Really?" He cocked his head at me. "Get on that side and pull."

No matter how hard we tried, the damn thing wasn't budging. Nathan pulled a little too hard because one of the springs broke off in his hand.

"Great." He rolled his eyes and I couldn't help but laugh.

He set down the spring and walked over to the bed and climbed in on the other side from where I had sat.

"Excuse me? What are you doing?"

"I can't sleep there, so I'm sleeping here." He smiled.

"The hell you are," I spoke as I put the cushions back on the couch. "There. All made up for you."

"You're crazy. I'm not sleeping on that couch. For one, it's not big enough, and two, sit on it and feel how hard it is."

I busted out into laughter again and he narrowed his eyes at me.

"You're drunk. I can't believe you right now."

"I'm not drunk. Maybe a little tipsy, but definitely not drunk."

He sighed as he took off his shirt and pulled the sheets up over him. "Good night, Fiona."

"You're breaking your rule about sleeping with someone in the same bed overnight."

"We didn't have sex, so it's different. You stay on your side and I'll stay on mine."

"That's right. You will stay on your side," I spoke as I pulled the extra pillows from the closet shelf and propped them up in between us.

Climbing into bed, I lay on my side, facing his direction with his back towards me. The pillows were low enough where I could see every defined muscle in his back. I studied them as well as his muscular arm, which rested over the sheet. I wanted to reach out and trace them, but I couldn't. Damn him for doing this to me. Closing my eyes, I finally fell asleep only to be woken up by the intense pressure in my bladder. Stumbling out of bed, I made my way to the bathroom, turned on the light, and sat down on the toilet. Reaching for the toilet paper, I screamed at the sight of, I kid you not, the largest and blackest spider I had ever seen. Spiders were my fear. Don't ask why because I couldn't tell you. I hated them and had near panic attacks whenever I saw one.

"What's wrong?" Nathan ran into the bathroom and looked at me as I jumped up from the toilet and cowered into the corner.

"A spider! Kill it! Hurry! It's crawling away!" I shouted as I pointed to it.

He grabbed a Kleenex from the sink and grabbed it, throwing it into the toilet.

"There, all gone. You can come out of the corner." He smirked.

"Are you sure it's gone?"

"Fiona, I flushed it. Come look for yourself."

I stretched my neck far enough to look down at the toilet to make sure it wasn't floating around.

"Thank you."

"You're that afraid of spiders?" he asked.

I swallowed hard. "Yes."

"What do you do at home when you're by yourself?"

"I keep a can of bug spray in every room of the house. When I see one, I spray it to death and then suck it up with the vacuum."

He let out a laugh as I stood there rubbing my shoulder, leaving the bathroom.

"What's wrong?"

"I was so tense, now my shoulder hurts."

He walked up behind me, placed his hands on my shoulders, and began massaging them.

"Relax. There's no need to be tense. The big bad spider is all gone."

I was tired and I didn't care if his hands were on me. They felt good, too good. If he kept it up, I was probably going to have an orgasm. I wanted one. I needed one. My heart was still racing and not from the spider.

"All better?" he whispered in my ear as he continued massaging me.

"Yes, but now I'm having some pain in my middle back."

"Right here?" he asked in a low voice as his hands moved down.

God, I was in heaven. "Yes. Right there." I was in a trance.

"Take off your shirt and lie face down on the bed," he spoke. "It'll be easier."

I didn't want him to stop because it felt incredibly good, so I took my shirt off and did as he asked, resting my head on my arms. He straddled me and began massaging my entire back. His strong hands manipulated me in every possible way. I felt his hard cock press against me. I knew damn well where this was going, but I was so relaxed, I didn't care. I was listening to my body and telling my brain to shut the fuck up.

"Do you want me to stop?" he asked.

"No," I moaned.

His fingers gripped the sides of my panties as he slowly pulled them down, while his tongue slid down my spine. After removing my panties, he spread my legs and dipped his finger inside me.

"You're so wet." He moaned as his lips pressed against my back.

I let out soft moans as he explored my insides. I'd deal with the aftermath of my emotions tomorrow. For now, I was taking in every bit of pleasure he was giving me. He climbed off of me, took down his pants, and rolled me onto my back. Our eyes locked onto each other's as he brushed my hair from my face. Without saying a word, he gently thrust inside me. Our eyes stayed fixed together as he slowly moved in and out of me. He lowered his head and brushed his lips against mine. My fingers dug into his back as our kisses became heated. His thrusting increased and I was on the verge of an orgasm.

"You feel so good," he spoke breathlessly as he broke our kiss. "I never want to stop making love to you."

My legs tightened around him as the wave of an orgasm flowed through my body. Letting out several moans, he pushed deep inside me one last time and halted, releasing himself inside me. He collapsed and swallowed hard while his fingers tangled through my hair.

Now what? I thought to myself. *He can't leave. I can't leave.* I was scared as a nervousness crept up inside me. He pulled out of me, threw the pillows in the middle of the bed on the floor, and told me to get under the covers. His tone was demanding.

I got under the covers as did he and he wrapped his arms around me and pulled me tightly into him. I could feel his heart beating a mile a minute. He had just entered into new territory and it appeared to have made him nervous as hell.

CHAPTER 37

Nathan

She was wrapped around me, her leg over mine. Her head lay on my chest as my arm held her all night. I was hesitant at first, my fears warranted. What kind of man would I be if I had just turned away from her? Did I care? Yes, I did care when it came to her.

She opened her eyes and looked up at me with a smile.

"Good morning," I spoke.

"Good morning. What time is it?"

I glanced over at the clock. "It's eight. The bank will be opening in about an hour."

Her hand glided over my chest and she let out a sigh.

"I'm nervous as to what is in that box."

"I'm a little nervous myself, but I'm sure it's no big deal."

She lifted her head and sat up, her beautiful breasts exposed and staring me in the face. My cock started to twitch.

"If it wasn't a big deal, he wouldn't have hidden the key and kept whatever is in that box here in Maine. He obviously didn't want anyone to find out what he was up to."

"Well." My fingers brushed against her breasts as I couldn't take my eyes off of them. "There's only one way to find out and that's to get up, get dressed, and unlock that box."

"Who's taking a shower first?" she asked with seriousness.

"We're going to have to take one together to save time." I smiled as I tugged at her hardened nipple.

"Then let's go." She grinned as she grabbed my hand.

After a thirty-minute shower, I wrapped a towel around my waist and she put on her robe. I needed to shave, so I stepped in front of the sink while she stood next to me and put on her makeup. We were sharing a space, something I had never done with a woman before. I kept stealing little glances as she made herself up. She didn't need makeup because I thought she was beautiful without it.

"Ouch!" I cut myself with the razor.

"Are you okay?" She looked over at me.

"Just cut myself and it's your fault." I winked.

"My fault?" She let out a light laugh. "How was it my fault?"

"Because you're distracting me." I grabbed a tissue and held it over my small cut.

She smiled as she applied her mascara. "Then keep your eyes to yourself."

"I'm trying." I grinned.

We headed down to the restaurant to grab a quick bite to eat and some coffee before going to the bank.

"We need to check out before we go," she spoke.

"Maybe we should reserve one more night. You never know what we're going to find in that safety deposit box. It's better to be safe than sorry."

"True."

After finishing breakfast, we headed to the front desk.

"Hello, how may I help you?" the same man from last night asked.

"We'd like to stay one more night," I spoke.

"What room are you in?"

"510."

"I'm sorry, but you reserved that for last night only and it's already booked for tonight."

"Seriously?" I asked in aggravation.

"It's tourist season, Mr. Carter."

"And I'm a tourist and I can't even get a damn room."

"I'm sorry."

"Check us out then, and we won't be coming back here," I huffed.

Fiona put her hand on my back and laughed. "Calm down. We'll be okay."

We climbed in the rental car and drove to the bank. It was a good thing they were open on a Saturday or else we would have had to stay until Monday and we would have been sleeping in the car.

Fiona

As we walked into the bank, I could feel my nerves getting the best of me.

"How may I help you?" an older woman asked.

"We need to get into our safety deposit box, please," I spoke.

"Name."

"Winslow." I pulled out the key.

"Follow me."

She took us to the vault where all the safety deposit boxes were located. She inserted her key and I inserted mine, turning them at the same time and hearing the lock click. She took the box out and led us to a small room.

"If you need anything else, just let me know." She smiled as she walked out and shut the door.

"Okay. Here we go." I took in a deep breath and opened the lid to the box.

Inside sat a white envelope. Removing it, I took out the folded piece of paper and looked at it.

"What the hell? This looks like a deed." I looked at Nathan, who took it from my hand.

"It is. It's a deed to some property your father purchased in a town called Mars Hill."

"How could he own property and not tell anyone?"

"I don't know. I think we need to go to Mars Hill."

"How the hell are we going to find the property? There's no address."

"We'd have to go to the registry office, but being it's Saturday, I'm sure they're closed. What the fuck?!" Nathan exclaimed as he took a closer look.

"What?"

"It says this land was purchased from my father, Thomas Carter." He stared blankly at me.

"Oh my God. Are you serious?"

"Yes. I'm very serious. He sold the property right before he died two years ago."

"And you didn't know anything about this?" I narrowed my eyes at him.

"No. And don't give me that look. I had no clue my father owned property in Maine. He didn't sell it through the company or else the deed would say Carter Management Group. This was a private transaction between the two of them."

He set down the deed and paced around the small room.

"Why would my father own property here and never speak of it? I just don't understand."

"I don't know, Nathan. There's so many questions that need to be answered."

"Let's go see what we can find out."

When we got back into the car, Nathan pulled up Mars Hill on the GPS.

"It's over a two-hour drive from here," he spoke. "Ready for a road trip?" He held out his hand to me.

"Ready." I smiled as I placed my hand in his.

Nathan was quiet for most of the ride and I could tell he was upset, so I didn't say too much. As we drove down the road, we approached a sign that said: Welcome to Mars Hill, population 1609.

"Damn, this is a small ass town," I spoke.

"It sure is."

"Where do we start?" I asked.

"I have no clue, but I'm hungry and I need a drink. Let's get something first."

"Okay, but where?" I laughed.

"There's a bar up ahead." He pointed. "We'll just stop there."

Pulling into the gravel parking lot of Fields Bar and Grill, we stepped inside and all heads turned to look at us.

"They know we're not from around here," I whispered.

"Of course they do. It's a small town. They know strangers when they see them."

"Welcome to Fields Bar and Grill." A young brunette girl smiled. "Just the two of you?"

"Yes," I replied.

She took us over to a table and placed our menus down in front of us. "Can I start you off with something to drink?"

"I'll have a scotch on the rocks. Make it a double."

"And I'll have a glass of merlot." I smiled.

"Coming right up."

I could feel the stares of the people around us and it was creeping me out.

"I thought small towns were supposed to be friendly," I leaned over and whispered to Nathan.

"I don't know. I've never really been to a small town like this before."

As we were looking over the menu, an older gentleman approached us.

"Good afternoon. Where you all from?" he asked.

"Los Angeles." Nathan smiled.

"What brings you to Mars Hill?"

Like it was any of this guy's business. What the hell? Are people not from this town allowed to eat here without being interrogated?

"We're just passing through," Nathan replied.

The waitress arrived to our table and set our drinks down in front of us.

"Where you going?" the nosy man asked.

"Nowhere in particular. We're just taking a road trip and seeing the beautiful sights your state has to offer."

"Are you ready to order?" the waitress asked.

"I'll have the lobster roll and an order of French fries, please." I smiled.

"I'll have the same," Nathan spoke as he handed her our menus.

"Good luck on your road trip. Enjoy your lunch." The man walked away.

"Okay, that was weird." I looked at Nathan as I picked up my glass of wine.

"He was just being friendly."

"Nosy is more like it." I took a sip and then looked down into my glass.

CHAPTER 38

Fiona

"What's wrong?" Nathan asked as he stared at me.

"Taste this wine." I handed him my glass.

"Wow." He looked at me in surprise.

"Right? This has to be the best glass of wine I have ever had in my life. Shit, Nathan. This is way better than Winslow Wines."

"I agree."

Our waitress came back and set our food down in front of us.

"Excuse me," I spoke. "Where do you get your wine?"

"We make it ourselves." She smiled.

"You make your own wine for this bar?"

"Yes. Our family owns the bar and we make our wines ourselves. We've been doing it for over forty years."

"It's very good. Do you grow your own grapes or do you have them shipped in?"

"We grow our own at our farm up the road."

"Well, it's the best wine I've ever had. Do you have other varieties?" I asked.

"Thank you and yes. We have Pino Grigio, Chardonnay, Moscato, Shiraz, and a Cabernet Sauvignon."

"I'll have a glass of each, please."

"Coming right up."

Nathan sat across from me with a frown splayed on his face.

"A glass of each? Are you out to get drunk or something?"

"I'm not going to drink the whole glass. I'm wine tasting." I smirked.

"Why?" He narrowed his eye at me. "What's going on in that head of yours?"

"Nothing. I like a good wine and I'm curious to see if the others are just as good as this merlot."

"We aren't here to wine taste."

"Shush," I spoke as I took a bite of my lobster roll.

The waitress came back and set the glasses of wine down in front of me.

"Thank you." I politely smiled.

I sipped from each glass and the wine got better and better.

"Holy shit, Nathan. Taste these."

"They're very good."

"Better than good and you know it." I pointed at him.

"Actually, this lobster roll is better than good." He smiled.

"Excuse me." I held up my finger at the waitress who was standing behind the bar.

"Yes?" She walked over.

"Is your wine available for purchase by the bottle?"

"No. We only make it and sell it by the glass here."

I gave her a dumbfounded look. "Why? Do you not know that this is probably the best wine on the market?"

"What's going on over here?" The nosy man from earlier walked up.

"This customer loves our wine and would like to buy bottles of it."

"We don't sell it by the bottle. May I ask your name?" He glared at me.

"My name is Fiona Winslow, and yours?" I held out my hand.

"Jim Fields, owner of this bar and wine." He lightly shook my hand.

"So you make this yourself?" I asked.

"Yes."

"On your farm up the road?"

"That's right."

"Have you ever considered marketing your wine and expanding to stores or restaurants?"

"No," he answered with a slight attitude.

"Actually, I did once, Miss Winslow," another older gentleman approached our table. "You'll have to excuse my son. We have different views on business. You wouldn't happen to be related to Chris Winslow?"

"Yes, he was my father."

"Was?"

"He passed away recently."

"I see. I'm sorry."

"Thank you. And you are?" I cocked my head as he took a seat at the table.

"Linden Fields. I'm the actual owner of this bar and the farm up the road."

"How do you know my father?"

"He came in here a couple of years ago, had a glass of wine, and offered me a business deal. He wanted us to produce wine for his company. Even purchased the land to grow another vineyard. Had me draw up some plans and said he needed to get the funds together to start building. He called me and said that he ran into a financial issue and that he'd be in touch as soon as he got it straightened out."

"How long ago was this?"

"Let's see. He purchased the land two years ago and the last I spoke with him was, probably, less than a year ago. I had no idea he passed away."

"Can we see your farm?" I asked. "Oh, I'm sorry. This is Nathan Carter."

The man looked at him oddly for a moment as Nathan extended his hand.

"Son of Thomas and Annie Carter?"

"You knew my parents?"

"Why, I'll be damned." He shook his hand. "The last time I saw you was when you were three years old."

"How did you know my parents?"

"Your mother and I were best friends. We grew up together."

"My mother grew up in Maine?"

"Yes. You didn't know that?"

"No. I didn't."

"She loved it here."

"Why did she leave?"

"Because your daddy came in and swept her off her feet." Linden smiled.

"But my father grew up in Los Angeles."

"I know. He was here with his family on vacation when they met. It was love at first sight. How can you not know any of this?"

"Because my father never spoke about my mother. He wouldn't. And every time I would ask a question about her, he told me that it didn't matter because she was gone."

My heart broke when I heard him say that because I could hear the sadness in his voice.

"Do you know where the land is that Mr. Winslow purchased from my father?"

"I do. It's right next to my farm and vineyard." He smiled. "If you're finished, I'll take you there, and don't worry about paying. It's on the house."

"Thank you, but I insist," Nathan spoke as he pulled out his wallet.

"No. Put your wallet away, son. It's on me."

CHAPTER 39

Nathan

Fiona and I climbed into the car and drove up the road to the see the land that my father sold to her father.

"I can't believe any of this," Fiona spoke.

"Me either."

"Are you okay?" she asked as she reached over and swept the back of her hand across my cheek.

"I'm fine," I replied in a serious tone.

Was I okay? I wasn't sure. Getting out of the car, we stood in front of the land that once belonged to my father.

"Twenty acres of pure beauty." Linden smiled.

"Why did my father buy this land in the first place?" I asked.

He turned to me and smiled. "It was an anniversary present for your mother. He knew how much she missed it here. Your father bought it because he was going to build a second home for them. He purchased it a year before she died, and by the time they had the house plans all drawn up, it was too late."

"Why did he hold on to it for so long?" I asked.

"Because it was the only piece of her he had left besides you."

Fiona took hold of my hand and held it.

"Why don't the two of you come on over to my house? I'll show you the vineyard and our winemaking equipment. You two are also staying for dinner. My wife Nancy would love to see you again, Nathan. Like I said, the last time we saw you was at your mother's funeral. By the way, how do you two know each other? You married? Dating?"

"No. We're not married or dating. I'm her business partner. I own part of Winslow Wines."

"I'll be damned. What a small world this is. Well, come on over and take a look at the vineyards."

Fiona

A part of me broke when I heard Nathan say that we weren't dating. I guess I was only sex to him and nothing else.

"So my father was going to build his own vineyard? I don't understand how you can grow wine grapes here in Maine with the winters you have."

"We can because of that." He pointed to one of the largest greenhouses I had ever seen.

After he showed us around the vineyard, we went up to his house where we met his wife, Nancy, and the four of us had a great home-cooked meal.

"Here's the plans your father and I drew up for the vineyard," Linden spoke as he laid the paper across the table.

"How did my father and Fiona's father meet?" Nathan asked.

"When her father came into the bar that day and we got to talking, he asked if there was any way to expand the vineyard. I knew that your father was still holding on to the land, so I called him and explained everything. The two of them flew out here together and made a deal. Your father was hesitant at first about selling, but after having a long talk with him, he agreed that there was no use holding on to it anymore."

CORPORATE ASSETS

"Do you know how much my father purchased the land for?" I asked.

"I think he purchased it for a million," Linden replied.

"Why would he keep this such a secret?" I asked Nathan.

"I have no clue."

"I do, I think," Linden spoke. "Your father wanted to brand this wine under a new company. From what he told me, the wine he already produced and sold was a higher end wine. He wanted to produce a cheaper wine."

"But why?" I asked.

"I don't know."

"Would you still be interested in what my father proposed to you?" I asked.

"I'd be willing to take another look." He smiled.

"Great. May I have your phone number?" I pulled out my phone as he rattled off his number. Pulling a piece of paper and pen from my purse, I wrote down my number and handed it to him. "Nathan and I will discuss everything and we'll get back with you."

"We better get going, Fiona. It's getting late. Thank you, Linden, for everything," Nathan spoke as he held out his hand.

"It was good to see you, Nathan, and it was a pleasure to meet you, Fiona."

"Same here." I smiled. "Thank you for dinner, Nancy." I gave her a hug.

"Any time. Don't be strangers."

We climbed into the car and I looked at Nathan.

"Now what? Where are we going?"

"Find a hotel around here," he spoke in a flat tone.

"There's a Hampton Inn about fourteen miles from here."

"Call and see if they have two rooms available."

"Okay," I spoke with an attitude as I made the call. "They have two rooms available."

"What's the address?" he asked.

As I rattled it off, he punched it into the GPS and began driving. When we arrived, we checked in. His room was on the third floor and mine was on the second. I was pissed as hell that he wanted his own room and I couldn't understand why. The elevator stopped on the second floor.

"This is my floor. I guess I'll see you in the morning," I spoke with disappointment.

"I'm having the plane come at ten a.m. So we'll have to leave here by seven thirty. Make sure you're ready."

The only thing I did was put my hand up and wave as I walked to my room. Upon opening the door, the smell of smoke and mildew smacked me in the face.

Ugh. I hated staying here alone. Damn Nathan Carter. I wanted to be with him because I knew all that talk about his mother and father bothered him. But obviously, he didn't want to be with me and it hurt. It hurt because I thought after what happened last night, things might have changed. He had shut me out and I didn't appreciate it. The way he held me all night after we made love was special, and now, I was dealing with the aftermath of his destruction on my emotional state.

After changing into my pajamas, I inspected the bed before I climbed into it. Grabbing my phone, I facetimed Lydia.

"Hey, you. How's Maine?"

"Eventful and challenging. It turns out my dad bought some land here to build his own vineyard."

"Wow. That's cool, right?"

"He bought it from Nathan's father."

"Say what?"

"It's a long story and I'll tell you when I get back."

"Where are you staying?"

"Hampton Inn."

"Ew, why?"

"It was the closest hotel to the town we were in."

"Where's Nathan? Isn't he staying with you?"

"We shared a room together last night at a different hotel and tonight he got us two rooms."

"Why?"

"To be honest, I don't really know. He's had an attitude with me since we found out that my dad bought his dad's land. How did things go with Will?"

A huge grin crossed her face.

"Wonderful. We went to dinner and to the movies and went to his place and had sex. I think I'm falling for him, Fiona."

"Slow down, Lydia. Don't assume or rush into anything. This isn't just about you anymore."

"I know, but we have a lot of fun together and so much in common. We're hanging out again tomorrow. Oh, I got some more freelance work and I'm revamping my website."

"That's great." I smiled. "I'm so happy everything's working out."

"Me too, but my insurance is still an issue. I'm covered for the next thirty days and after that in order to keep it, I'll have to pay COBRA and it's an arm and a leg. I was checking into private insurance and the coverage isn't as good."

"Keep looking. I'm sure you'll find something comparable. I'm going to go. I just wanted to check in. I love you."

"I love you too. Have a safe trip home."

After ending the call, I turned on the TV for a while. As I was watching *Law and Order*, the only thing that was on, something caught my attention out of the corner of my eye. Two big black spiders crawling down the wall, as if they were playing follow the leader.

"Oh hell no!" I yelled as I jumped out of bed, grabbed my phone and my bag, ran out of the room, and up to Nathan's.

I pounded on the door until he opened it.

"Fiona, what the hell are you doing?"

"I need the keys to the rental car."

"Why?"

"Because I'm sleeping in it tonight. I'd rather sleep in there than in this bug-infested hotel."

"What are you talking about? Get in here." He took hold of my hand and pulled me inside.

"There were not one, but two big black hairy spiders crawling down the wall across from my bed. Keys, please." I held out my hand.

"You are not sleeping in the car. We'll switch rooms."

Asshole.

He grabbed his bag and I handed him my room key.

"I'll see you in the morning," he spoke as he walked out the door.

I stood there in shock as the door shut. I wasn't expecting that. I expected him to stay here with me, not go off and take my room. I was too mad to go to sleep. All I'd do was toss and turn all night, so I took my iPad from my bag, and before climbing into bed, I searched every inch of the room for spiders. I stayed up until two a.m. doing research and taking notes.

CHAPTER 40

Nathan

I couldn't share a room with Fiona because I needed to think. Hearing what Linden said about my parents brought back a lot of memories of my father. I wanted to be alone and I knew I probably hurt her, but I hoped she would understand. If I would have told her that I wanted to be alone, she would have flooded me with a million questions and I didn't want to deal with that.

Grabbing my bag, I went up to her room and knocked on the door. There was no answer, so I knocked again. Pulling my phone from my pocket, I sent her a text message.

"I'm at your door. Why aren't you answering?"

"Because I'm waiting for you in the lobby."

Rolling my eyes, I put my phone back in my pocket and headed downstairs.

"Why are you down here?"

"Why not? You didn't say where we'd meet," she spoke as we headed to the rental car.

"I just assumed you would have waited for me in your room."

"You know what they say about people who assume," she spoke.

I could already tell that this was going to be a long two-hour drive back to Bangor and an even longer flight home.

As soon as we got in the car, Fiona put her earphones in and turned on her music. I kept glancing over at her, but she wouldn't look at me. She was definitely pissed about last night. Reaching over, I pulled one of her earphones from her ear.

"What do you think you're doing?" She glared at me.

"Are you just going to sit there and not speak to me the whole way home?"

"I have nothing to say. If I did, I would talk." She looked out the window.

"You're pissed at me for last night. Aren't you?"

"Please." She put her hand up. "Why would I be pissed?"

"Because I got us two rooms and then wouldn't stay with you when you came up to my room because of the spiders in yours."

"The only reason we shared a room the other night was because it was the only room available. I didn't expect us to share again."

"I don't believe you. If you weren't pissed, you would be talking. You always talk. You love to talk."

"So what are you saying? That I talk too much?"

"No. I'm not saying that at all." I reached over and pinched her cheek.

"Do that again, Mr. Carter, and you won't have a hand left."

I couldn't help but smile at her. "Just admit you're mad at me."

"Give me an explanation of your behavior last night and then I'll let you know." She arched her brow.

"I just wanted to be alone. I had a lot of things to process about what Linden said about my parents and I knew if I told you that, you'd flood me with questions."

"I would not have."

"Yes, you would have. You're a woman and women ask way too many questions."

"You're sexist."

"I'm honest." I smirked.

"I will admit that I was a little upset, but what upsets me more is the fact that you thought I would ask too many questions."

"I'm sorry."

"Apology accepted. Now, if you'll excuse me, I have some music to listen to."

"Don't you want to talk?" I asked as she put her earphone back in her ear.

"I'm afraid if we do, I'll ask too many questions. So it's probably best we don't for a while."

I sighed as she turned her head and stared out the window. She was still mad.

We arrived at the airport, turned in the rental car, and boarded the plane. The minute we took our seats, Fiona pulled out a few pieces of paper with writing all over them and her iPad. I leaned over to get a better look at what she had written and she slowly turned her head and glared at me.

"Can I help you?"

"What do you have there?" I asked.

"Why?"

"Because if it's business related, I ought to know about it." I raised my brow.

"I was up all night doing research and I'm putting together a plan for our new wine line."

"New wine line?"

"Yes. The one my father was going to do."

"Would you like to explain it to me?" I asked in irritation.

"Not really."

"Damn it, Fiona!" I snapped. "Enough with your attitude! I already apologized to you for last night. Now drop it and move on! This is the reason I don't get involved in relationships!" I growled.

"We aren't in a relationship, Nathan. I'm your business partner. If you would like to dissolve that partnership, I'm willing to listen," she spoke calmly.

She really knew how to push my buttons.

"I will explain my concept and plan when I'm finished. Until then, you're just going to have to wait."

I clenched my fists as my breathing became rapid. Taking out my iPad, I turned it on and started playing a game to calm the fuck down. I was not going to let her get to me.

Fiona

I was over it and over him. Okay, maybe not totally over him, but I was sure as hell trying. Developing this new wine line was the most important thing right now and I couldn't lose focus. He was straightforward with me about relationships and dating and I got the message loud and clear. This game was over.

We had been up in the air for about two hours when I was ready to reveal my plan to him. He was sitting on the couch, playing on his iPad when I got up from my seat and walked over to him.

"I'm ready."

"Okay," he spoke while still looking at his iPad.

"Women drink way more wine than men do. It's become their social obligation to consume a glass or two every day or night while alone or with girlfriends. Women are far more stressed than men and, therefore, turn to the lovely beverage for relaxation."

That grabbed his attention.

"And why are women more stressed than men?" he asked in a cocky way.

"They worry more. The pressure to rise in the corporate world, family stress, kids running around all day screaming, friendship woes, self-esteem issues, husbands/boyfriends, and the day to day grind of trying to get everything done. Women worry more and focus too much on the stress. Men just use their flight or fight senses. Women are expected to hold down jobs, raise a family, cook, clean, do laundry, grocery shop, while men leave in the morning for the office, come home to a home-cooked meal, and then sit down with their feet up, ignoring what's going on around them."

"Stop right there!" He pointed at me. "Men are equally stressed. They're expected to bring home the money and provide the kind of lifestyle the woman wants so she can go spend all his hard earned money like it's water."

"Women do two things when they're stressed. They shop and drink wine. Wine relaxes them. Men, on the other hand, use sex with other women to release their stress or hit the bar for a bottle of beer or a glass of scotch or bourbon. So, my point is, we need to thank the men that create such stress in women's lives because it drives them to drink wine!" I smiled.

"And you call me a sexist?"

"Shut up, Nathan, and just listen."

He draped his arm over the back of the couch with a smug look on his face.

"It's a given. Women buy and consume more wine than men do. So I want this new wine line to appeal to women. They buy the cheap stuff because they drink so much of it; they aren't going to spend big bucks on it when they go through so much. Men lean towards the more expensive wine, a.k.a. Winslow Wines. Now, we can make cheap wine through Linden and his existing vineyard, which is great and would be very profitable. We take the land my father owns, cultivate it, build on it, and create a magical vineyard. Because, let me tell you," I pointed at him, "once women get a taste of Fiona Rose Wine, they'll be begging for more."

"Fiona Rose Wine?" His brow arched.

"Yes. The name of our subsidiary wine company. We'll take the funds from Winslow Wines and invest in the subsidiary company, and as soon as that company pulls in a profit, we'll put it back into Winslow."

"Why Fiona Rose?"

"Why not?" I frowned. "Do you have a problem with my name?"

"No. I didn't know Rose was your middle name. It's kind of classy. I think I like it."

"Of course it's classy. I'm a classy woman." I smiled.

"A classy woman who intentionally smashes up beautiful cars to get back at her boyfriend." He smirked.

"Right." I brushed it off with a smile. "I can see it now." I raised my hands. "A bottle of Fiona Rose sitting proudly on the counters of every American home, waiting to be opened and drunk by those oh-so stressed women who are desperately in need of some relaxation without the worry of another person's needs or wishes. All they need is a good glass of vino to curl up on the couch with."

He rolled his eyes.

"So I'm going to have Lydia design the label. A label that will appeal to women. A label that speaks of relaxation and comfort. I'll need you to put the numbers together for Linden. What do you think?"

"I think it's a possible idea."

"No. No." I shook my finger. "It is a profitable idea. One that will put Winslow Wines back on its feet."

"So you're planning on sticking with Tobias Vineyards for the grapes for Winslow Wines?" he asked.

"Just for the time being until we can find another vineyard. Or better yet, we'll build our own for Winslow Wines."

"One project at a time, Fiona. What about marketing for Fiona Rose?"

"Don't you worry about that. Marketing is my expertise. I can market any product with great success."

"You're a little full of yourself." He smirked.

"I'm a damn good marketer, so I can say that."

"Okay. I'm on board. I like the idea and I'll work on a proposal for Linden. But we still have to concentrate on Winslow Wines."

"I know, and I am. Don't you worry about that."

CHAPTER 41

Nathan

I didn't feel bad anymore for last night. If I hadn't done what I did, she wouldn't have researched and come up with a plan. I sat there, trying to calm my cock because all her business talk was turning me on. I wanted to rip off that sundress she was wearing and fuck her right here on the couch. But I was afraid to even suggest it or make a move. I wasn't too sure she was over what happened yet.

After we landed back in L.A., we climbed in the limo and took Fiona back to Winslow Wines to pick up her car.

"Would you like to grab some dinner?" I asked.

"No thanks. I'm just going to go home and curl up with a glass of wine. We have a sacred relationship." She smirked as she climbed into her car. "Have a good night, Nathan." She waved as she drove away.

I stood there with my hands tucked in my pants pockets, shaking my head. That woman was crazy and she drove me nuts. But it was her craziness that I found so attractive and made me want her more and more every day.

I was sitting at my desk working up a proposal for Linden, when Will walked in.

"Welcome back. How was Maine?"

"It was okay. Fiona wants to start a subsidiary company and sell a cheaper wine tailored to women."

"What do you think?"

"I don't know. It sounds like a good idea, but I hate marketing something to a specific gender."

"Well, knowing what I know about Fiona, it doesn't matter what you hate. She's going to do it anyway."

I sighed. "I know that. How are things with you and Lydia?"

"Things are great." He grinned. "She's an animal in the bedroom and just an overall sweet girl. I really like her. We'll see how things go. I'm afraid to ask how things are with you and Fiona."

I shrugged. "I pissed her off and now she won't drop the attitude, even though I apologized."

"You, Nathan Carter, apologized to a woman?" His brow raised.

"Very funny. Now get out of here. I have work to do."

He chuckled and walked to the door. "Oh, by the way, don't forget that business conference is this Friday night."

"I did forget. Thanks for reminding me."

After he left, I picked up my phone and started to dial Fiona, then stopped and placed my phone in my pocket as I got up from my chair. I wanted to see her and see what she was up to, so I decided to stop by the office.

"Jerry, you've been stocking our wine for the past ten years. Yes, I know things have been bad with us, but I'm telling you I've taken over and things are back on track. You won't be disappointed. We've been your number one selling wine for years. Are you just going to give that up because of a mistake my father made? People make mistakes, Jerry. But I can promise you that things are better now. I trust you to sell my wine. Now I need you to trust me to do my job. If not, I'm sure that liquor store that just opened up around the block from you would love to sell my wine. I'm sure they're your biggest competitor right now. Great. You've made the right decision. If you have any problems, you call me directly. I will always be here for you. Bye, Jerry."

"Bravo." I clapped my hands. "I'm assuming you got a vendor back?"

"So far, that makes ten. Is there something I can do for you?"

"There's always something you can do for me, beautiful, but I'm here to ask if you're going to the business conference Friday night at the Beverly Hills Hotel?"

"I know nothing about a business conference. Josh!" she shouted.

"Yes, Madame Winslow?"

"Do you know anything about a business conference at the Beverly Hills Hotel this Friday night?"

"Yes. Have you not gone through your mail, in like weeks?" He frowned.

She rummaged through the pile that was sitting on her desk.

"Oh. Here it is. I'm not sure."

"I think you should go," I spoke as I stood in front of her desk with my hands in my pockets.

"Why?" She narrowed her eye at me.

"Because there will be a lot of influential people there, vendors and business connections. It may be a good idea to put a bug in some of their ears about the new wine line."

"Good idea. I'll go."

"You'll go with me." I smiled. "After all, I am your business partner and we should go together."

"So you keep reminding me." She sighed. "Fine. We can go together, but as business partners, understand?"

"What else would we go as? I have to go." I turned and headed towards the door.

"Is that all you wanted?"

"For now." I winked.

I was sexually frustrated. More so than I had ever been my entire life and it was driving me crazy. All I could think about was Fiona and her beautiful naked body underneath me as I pounded into her.

"Hey, Nathan." Will walked into my office.

"WHAT!" I snapped at him.

"Whoa. What's wrong?" he asked.

I sighed as I got up from my desk and poured myself a scotch. "Nothing."

"Something's wrong. I can tell. You normally don't snap like that."

"You really want to know what's wrong? I'm sexually frustrated at the moment." I threw back my drink.

"Okay. Get out your little black book and call someone up. You know any one of them would be happy to take care of your needs."

"I don't want anyone in my little black book. I want to have sex with Fiona and Fiona only."

"Then go have sex with her." He gave me a confused look.

"She won't. She still has an attitude with me about the other night."

"Listen, Nathan, you know I've always had your back and I always will. You've got it bad for Fiona and for reasons I'm unsure of, you're fighting yourself. Just tell her how you feel about her. I know you've never been one to talk about your feelings, but maybe she's the one you should be opening up to."

"I can't."

"Then, my friend, you're going to lose her. She's not going to stick around waiting for you to get your shit together. Like I said before, it's time we grew up. Anyway, now I forgot why I came in here."

Fiona

I left the office early and headed home where Lydia was meeting me to go over label ideas. She said she already had done some mock ups from what I told her I was thinking of and I couldn't wait to see them.

As soon as I walked through the door, I kicked off my shoes and headed straight to the kitchen for a glass of wine. Tough day equaled wine. As I was changing out of my business clothes, I heard Lydia's voice downstairs.

"Fi, I'm here."

"I'll be down in a minute," I yelled from my room.

When I got downstairs, I poured Lydia a glass of iced tea, grabbed my wine, and we sat in the living room talking over ideas for the wine labels.

"I love this concept." I smiled as I viewed her mock ups. "I think they'll look great on the wine bottles."

"Thanks. Do you think Nathan will like them?"

"Who cares what he likes. It's my idea, my company, and my decision."

"You're still mad at him for the other night?"

"No. I'm just over him in general. I'm not being used anymore. The only thing I'm good for to him is sex."

"I'm sure that's not true. Will told me, and don't you dare repeat this, that he thinks Nathan really likes you for more than just a business partner and friend."

"Yeah. He likes me as a sex toy." I frowned.

"Well, maybe that too, but Will said that Nathan doesn't know how to express his feelings."

"Oh well. Listen, Lydia, I don't want to talk about Nathan Carter. I just want to get moving on this wine line so I can repay the money he invested in Winslow Wines and get my company back."

"You know you're in love with him. I can see it all over that pretty little face of yours." She smirked.

"Doesn't matter how I feel about him. He can never return the feelings. He's the wrong man for me and I need to remember that."

CHAPTER 42

*F*iona

It had been a couple of days since I'd heard from Nathan, and to be honest, it made me sad. Yes, I know what I said, but the truth was I missed him. Even though he annoyed me ninety-nine percent of the time, I liked being in his company, even if he only viewed me as something to have sex with. I missed sex with him, and if I could turn off my emotions and feelings, it would be easy. But I couldn't. I was an intelligent being with the emotions of a love struck moron. Sometimes, I wished I'd been born a guy so I didn't have to go through the painstaking emotional process.

I glanced at the redhead who was staring at me from across the room. Damn that picture. I laid my forehead down on my desk.

"Why is it every time I come in here, you're laying your head down? Do you ever do any work?" Nathan spoke.

Lifting my head, I watched his fine ass walk over and take a seat behind his desk.

"I work my ass off. I was taking a break."

"I flew out to Maine a couple of days ago and presented the deal to Linden and he accepted. He is now officially producing wine for

Fiona Rose Wine Company. You did have the attorneys file the paperwork, right?"

"Yes. Uncle Robbie took care of all of that."

"Good."

"I have the label designs from Lydia."

"How long have you had them?" he asked.

"A few days."

"And you couldn't bother to show me?"

"I hadn't heard from you."

"And you can't call me, why?" He frowned.

"I was busy."

"I see. Since I'm here, I'll take a look at them now."

Picking up the designs from my desk, I walked them over to Nathan. He stared at them for a moment and then looked up at me.

"They're good. Definitely geared towards women only. So will each type of wine have a different label?"

"Yes."

"I need to tell you something," he spoke with a serious tone.

"What?"

"We're holding off on the vineyard plans."

"Why?"

"I think we shouldn't jump into anything. Linden can supply us with what we need to start Fiona Rose and I think we should wait and see how that goes first."

"It's going to go great, Nathan. Besides, we can use the vineyard for other wines as well."

"I hate to break the news to you, but I'm not so sure how well wine that's produced in Maine is going to do. Now, if the vineyard was in Sonoma, Napa, or even France, it would stand a better chance."

"You're a wine sexist."

"A what?" He cocked his head.

"You think that good wine can only be made in California or Europe."

"Not true. I just don't want to invest the money if this isn't going to work. You need to understand that, Fiona."

"I do understand, Nathan." I grabbed the designs out of his hands. "I understand that you don't trust me."

"This isn't about you, Fiona. This is about business."

"I can make this work. With the right marketing, this wine will do better than Winslow ever did."

"Well, we'll have to wait and see."

"Fine." I turned my back and sat down at my desk. "Are you finished?"

"Yes. I'll pick you up tomorrow at five o'clock for the business conference."

"Fine."

"Is that all you can say?"

"I could say 'fuck you,' but I'm not sure you'd want me to."

"I'd take a fuck from you." He smirked.

"OUT, NOW!" I pointed to the door.

As soon as he walked out of the office, the anger inside got the best of me. I got up from my chair and yelled down the hall.

"Those days are over, Mr. Carter. Move on!"

"I already have, Miss Winslow," he shouted back.

"UGH!" I slammed my office door shut, walked over to the redhead, threw her on the floor, and began stomping on her with my heels, leaving several holes through the portrait.

"Someone forgot to take their crazy pills today," Josh spoke as he opened the door.

"Leave me alone, Josh." I began to cry and sank down to the floor.

"Hey." He walked over, sat down next to me, and began rubbing my back. "You're in love with him, aren't you?"

I nodded my head as the tears poured from my eyes. "I'm so stupid. God, I hate myself right now. I always fall for the wrong men. What the hell is the matter with me?"

"Nothing is the matter with you, Fiona. It's them who have the problem."

"You think?" I sniffled as I looked at him.

"I know. You're a beautiful and smart woman. Probably one of the smartest women I know, and if I wasn't gay, I'd totally fall for you." He smiled.

"Really?"

"Really. Now pick yourself up, hold your head high, and be that confident, strong woman I work so hard for. Don't ever let a man get you down. You're too good for that."

"Thanks, Josh." I gave a small smile.

I had a momentary lapse of insanity. Getting up off the floor, I picked up the redhead and hung her back on the wall, holes and all. Grabbing my phone, I dialed Linden.

"Hello."

"Linden, it's Fiona Winslow."

"Hey, Fiona, how are you?"

"I'm great. Listen, how soon can we expect a first shipment?"

"About a month."

"Okay. I've already selected the bottles and I'm having them shipped out to you along with the labels."

"Great, as soon as we get them, we'll bottle up each brand and send them right to you for approval."

"Thanks, Linden."

CHAPTER 43

*N*athan

She couldn't get pissed off like that every time I did something she didn't like. Maybe investing in her company wasn't the smartest idea after all. She told me to move on. If that was how she felt, then maybe it was time I did. But there was a part of me that couldn't. Damn her! This wasn't like me. I hated this. Hearing her say those words was like a knife slowly going into my heart. If I let myself do what I swore I'd never do, it would destroy me, just like it did my father.

*F*iona

I hadn't heard from Nathan since I kicked him out of the office yesterday afternoon.

"Show me your dress, sweetheart," Jose spoke as he stood in my bedroom.

Grabbing my short black lace V-neck dress from the closet, I held it up.

"Oh. Very sexy. I love it. You'll need to wear your hair up. I have the perfect hairstyle that will look fabulous on you."

"Thanks for coming on such short notice. I appreciate it."

"No problem, sweetheart. Now sit down in the chair and let me work my magic." He smiled.

After Jose pinned up my hair, he applied my makeup.

"All finished." He grinned.

I looked at the time. It was four fifty. Nathan was going to be here in ten minutes. Getting up from the chair, I slipped into my short black dress and put on my stiletto black heels. Looking into the full-length mirror, I smiled.

"You look amazing, Fiona. Every man at that business conference is going to be wondering what you have on under that sexy dress."

"Thanks, Jose. As always, you've outdone yourself."

The doorbell rang and I still needed to find some jewelry to wear.

"That's Nathan. Can you go let him in and tell him I'll be down in a minute."

※

Nathan

The door opened and instead of Fiona standing there, there was some tanned-looking guy with his black hair pulled back into a ponytail.

"You must be Nathan." He stuck out his hand.

"Yes. And you are?" I raised my brow.

"Jose. Hair and makeup artist extraordinaire." He smiled.

"Nice to meet you." I shook his hand and stepped inside.

"Fiona said she'll be down in a minute."

Placing my hands in my pants pockets, I strode into the living room. As soon as I heard the clicking of heels coming down the stairs, I turned around, and instantly, my heart stopped beating.

"You look stunning." I smiled.

"Thank you. So do you." She smiled back.

Okay. This was a good sign. I didn't sense an attitude from her. Jose followed her down with his suitcase in hand and gave her a light hug.

"Have fun at the ball, princess," he spoke.

"Thank you, Jose. I will."

"Are you ready?" I asked.

"I am." She nodded.

I held out my arm to her and she dismissed it and walked ahead of me. Rolling my eyes, I sighed. Maybe the attitude I sensed was gone wasn't. I climbed in the limo on the other side of her and offered her a glass of wine. She was gorgeous and my cock was misbehaving like a kid in a toy store. I couldn't help but stare at her long slender legs as she crossed them, remembering what it was like when they were tightly wrapped around my waist multiple times.

She took the glass from my hands and took a sip, leaving a perfect lip print on the rim. Fuck. I wanted her so badly right here and right now.

"Lydia called and told me that Will invited her to come along tonight. He felt maybe she could drum up some business."

"Yeah. He told me," I spoke. "It seems the two of them have really hit it off."

"Yep. She really likes him and he really likes her. That's what he told her. It's amazing how two people can get along when they express how they feel for each other. I mean, they haven't known each other that long."

"No, they haven't." I stirred uncomfortably in my seat.

"It must have been an instant connection," she spoke.

I needed to change the subject and quick. She was itching to start something by saying what she did.

"Did you get the labels off to the printers?" I asked.

"Yes. They'll be ready in a couple of days as well as the bottles. They're being shipped out to Linden and as soon as he gets them, he said he'll bottle up each brand and send it to me for approval."

"Great. I can't wait to see how they look."

"Me either."

As soon as we arrived at the Beverly Hills Hotel, I climbed out of the car and opened the door for Fiona before Jason had a chance to. Holding out my hand to her, she surprisingly took it and I helped her from the car. There was no way I was letting this night end without her in my bed. No way in hell.

CHAPTER 44

*F*iona

Grabbing a glass of champagne from the tray, I saw Will and Lydia across the room.

"OMG, you're gorgeous." Lydia smiled as we hugged. "Damn, Jose did your hair and makeup perfectly."

"Thank you. You look gorgeous as well."

"Hello, Fiona." Will smiled as he kissed my cheek.

"Hi, Will. It's nice to see you again."

Nathan walked over and placed his hand on the small of my back. I stiffened at the soft touch of his fingers. Fingers that made my body explode every time he touched me.

"Oh look, it's Bryce and his wife. Oh, and Bryce's wife is talking to his mistress. Interesting. I think a proper hello is in order." I smiled.

"Fiona, don't." Nathan lightly grabbed hold of my arm.

"Don't worry. I'll be nice." I winked as I walked in their direction and Nathan followed.

"Trudy, Celia. Hi." I gave the biggest fake award-winning smile ever.

"Fiona. You look pretty." Celia smiled.

"Nice to see you, Fiona." Trudy hugged me. "It's been way too long. I'm so sorry about your father."

"Thank you. I appreciate it."

"I was shocked to hear that you turned down the promotion Bryce gave you."

Bryce walked up behind his wife and Celia with a frightened look upon his face.

"Fiona." He smiled.

"Hello, Bryce. It's so good to see you." I lightly hugged him. "Your wife was just telling me how shocked she was that I turned down the promotion you gave me."

"Umm. Yes. She was." He glared at me as my lips curved upwards. "I told her that you were a great loss to the company and I'd wished you would reconsider, but then your father passed away and you took over his company. By the way, how's that going for you?"

"It's going great. Actually, I do have some business to discuss with you, so would you mind?" I cocked my head and gave him a look, telling him he had no choice.

"No. Not at all. Trudy, we'll be right back," he spoke.

"No worries, darling." She smiled.

I led Bryce a few feet away from his wife and mistress and Nathan followed behind. I could see the look of worry across his face.

"What do you want to discuss?" Bryce asked in irritation.

"I want you to pay for Lydia's insurance for the next eighteen months."

"What? You're crazy."

"*I'm* crazy? You have both your mistress and wife here. Gee, Bryce, that's really risky. I would hate for something to slip out of my mouth to Trudy about how I was passed up for the promotion and Celia got it because you're fucking her."

"Fiona," Nathan spoke.

"Stay out of it, Nathan. This doesn't concern you."

"You wouldn't dare. Because if you did, I would destroy you."

I let out a light laugh. "You would destroy me? No, darling, I would destroy you. By the way, does Celia know about your little hotel visits with Samantha from the finance department?"

He looked around. "How the fuck do you know about that?" he spoke through gritted teeth.

"Just because I no longer work for your pathetic company doesn't mean I don't know what's going on." I smiled devilishly. "Poor Trudy. If only she knew what her husband was doing during and after business hours. Seems to me like you've dug yourself a grave, Bryce."

"Fine. I'll pay for Lydia's insurance, but she cannot tell anyone. If word got out that I was doing that for her, then everyone I laid off would want it too and they could sue me."

"You're such a sweet guy for doing that for Lydia and her baby." I placed my hand on his chest. "She'll be so happy and I know she'll promise not to say a word about it. You can trust both of us, Bryce." I winked. "Enjoy the conference." I walked away and Nathan followed.

"I've got to hand it to you, Fiona. You never cease to amaze me. How did you know about the other girl?"

"I had Josh do some stalking after Bryce fired Lydia." I smiled.

He just shook his head as he kicked back his drink. He went off to talk to some business friends of his and I went off to do some mingling and business talk of my own. It was a great evening so far and I was happy I decided to attend. I talked a lot about Fiona Rose Wine and even got some interested prospects who were excited to jump on board. I was doing this and I was proud of myself. I ended up speaking with James Henderson. He worked for a handbag company and I was in charge of their marketing. We had worked closely together and he was always flirting with me, trying to get me to go out with him, even though he was engaged to be married. Douchebag.

"It's good to see you again, Fiona." He smiled.

"Nice to see you too, James. How are you?"

He shrugged. "I'm okay. Wendy and I broke off the engagement and broke up. It just wasn't working out."

"I'm sorry to hear that."

"I'm not." He grinned. "So." He lightly ran his finger up my arm. "How about going out for a drink?"

"We already have our drinks." I held up my glass as I pulled my arm away.

"You know what I mean." His fingers stroked my cheek.

"No, actually, I don't, James, and I really think you need to stop touching me like that."

"Come on, Fiona. I know you were always into me. The only reason you declined my advances was because of Wendy."

"Not true, James. I declined your advances because I wasn't into you."

"One night with me and I can promise you'd be into me." He smirked as he placed his hand on top of mine and I pulled away.

"Sorry, James. But it's a no. I'm not dating anyone right now and that's how I like it."

"So what are you doing for sex? Wait, I bet you get yourself off every night. Am I right? That is so sexy."

"Good bye, James."

As I began to walk away, he grabbed my arm with force and yanked me back to him.

"What the fuck are you doing?" I snapped at him.

"I want you, Fiona. I bet you like it rough." He smiled.

"Let go of me." I tried to get out from his tight grip.

"Get your fucking hand off of her now!" Nathan yelled as he threw a punch at him and sent him to the ground. "Come near her again and you won't live to see another day!" he spoke through gritted teeth as he reached down and grabbed hold of his shirt.

"Are you okay?" He looked at me as the crowd of people stood there staring at us.

"I'm fine!" I huffed as I stormed out of the hotel.

"What is your problem?!" he shouted as he followed me outside.

"I don't need you to save me, Nathan! I could have handled him myself!" I climbed into the back of the limo.

"Yeah. It really looked like you were handling it." He slid in next to me.

"You caused a scene in there in front of everyone!"

"He caused the scene when he grabbed you like that! Nobody, and I mean nobody, touches you that way." He pointed his finger at me.

"Maybe I liked it! You may be part owner of my company, but you do not own me!"

He sat there in a rage, shaking his head while staring out the window.

"You liked it, eh?" he mumbled.

I didn't speak another word the whole way home. I was furious with him for doing what he did. As soon as Jason pulled to the curb of my condo, I opened the door and got out as fast as I could. Fumbling in my purse for my keys, I unlocked the door and before I knew it, Nathan grabbed hold of my arm and pushed me inside, shutting the door behind him.

"What the fuck do you think you're doing?"

"You liked it? Is that what you want?" He grabbed my wrists with one hand and pinned me up against the wall, shoving his hand up my dress and pushing my panties to the side while his mouth devoured my neck.

"Nathan," I spoke breathlessly.

His fingers dipped inside me with force and I let out a low moan. I couldn't stop him. He was too strong. I didn't want to stop him.

"Tell me to stop and I will." He stared into my eyes as his fingers moved inside me. "Do you want me to stop, Fiona?"

There was something in his eyes that bothered me. It wasn't rage but sadness. It was almost as if he was begging me not to tell him no.

"No. I don't want you to stop."

His mouth smashed into mine as our kiss deepened and our tongues once again welcomed each other with joy. My body tightened as the wave of an orgasm hit, leaving me gasping for air and wanting to collapse to the ground. Nathan let go of my wrists and brought my arms down and then picked me up and carried me upstairs, where he slowly took off my dress and panties. Kneeling down, his mouth explored my lower half as my hands raked through his hair. He stood up and quickly stripped out of his clothes while I pulled back the sheets and climbed into bed. He hovered over me, his lips gently touching mine before traveling to each breast, sucking and nipping seductively at my nipples. I felt no greater pleasure than when I was with him.

I let out a gasp and tilted my head back as he thrust into me, burying every inch of his rock hard cock deep inside. His low moans of satisfaction excited me. There was something different about the way he made love to me. He was slow and gentle as if he was savoring every stroke. His fingers interlaced with mine and he brought them over my head as my body released another orgasm. The soft subtle moans that escaped my lips held him in place as he came inside me.

"I'm sorry, Fiona," he whispered as he buried his face into the side of my neck.

"For what?"

He didn't speak a word as he climbed off of me and rolled onto his back.

"Are you okay?" I asked as I stroked his chest.

"I'm okay." He looked at me and brushed my hair away from my face.

I needed to use the bathroom, so I got up and told him that I'd be right back. A funny feeling crept up inside me. I couldn't explain exactly what it was. As soon as I was finished, I walked back to the bedroom and he was gone. Putting on my robe and walking downstairs, I went into the kitchen to see if maybe he went to get a drink of water and he wasn't there. Looking out the window, the limo was nowhere to be seen. He was gone, and in that moment, I felt like I had died. For the first time in my life, I could feel the breaking of my heart. The physical pain was unlike anything I'd ever felt before. Tears started to fall down my face as I sat down on the couch and curled into a fetal position, holding on to the decorative pillow that sat next to me.

It felt like I had been crying for hours, when in fact, it had only been fifteen minutes. All kinds of thoughts raced through my head. The questions and no answers. Answers I desperately needed if I was going to make it through this. Getting up from the couch, I dried my eyes. My crying spell was done for now because I was angry. How dare he do this to me. Rage consumed me and gave me strength. I ran up the stairs to my room, went into the closet, and threw on a pair of yoga pants and a tank top. When I climbed into my car, I opened up the tracking app on my phone to see where he was. He was home and that was exactly where I was headed.

CHAPTER 45

Nathan
My biggest fear consumed me and that was the reason I left. I knew what I did would hurt her, and after what I had done, she'd never be able to forgive me and it would be the end of a friendship forever. I didn't want to lose her, but I had to let her go. The fear that resided inside me was too strong for me to control.

I kicked back one drink after another, trying to drown my sorrows away. There was a loud knock at the door. When I opened it, Fiona was standing there, eyes red and swollen from the tears that I had caused her to cry. I should have expected this.

"How dare you!" She pushed me back and forced her way inside my home. "How dare you do what you did. Why, Nathan?" she shouted.

I didn't know what to say because she wouldn't understand why I left. So I just stood there.

"Do you know how much you've hurt me? Or is it that you just don't care? Is there one ounce of feeling in that heart of stone of yours?"

I couldn't answer.

"ANSWER ME!" she screamed at the top of her lungs.

Seeing her like this broke me. I stood there, my fists clenched, battling the demons inside.

"I never want to see you again, Nathan Carter," she spoke. "If you want my company, you can have it because I'm selling my shares and I'm moving as far away from this place as I can get. You have destroyed me and I'm not sure how long it'll take for me to put myself back together. Maybe you don't want to hear this, but I fell in love with you and I thought maybe you felt something for me too other than a good fuck. But I was wrong. Have a nice life, Nathan." She stormed past me and headed for the door.

"You weren't wrong!" I shouted to get her attention.

She stopped dead in her tracks, her back turned to me.

"I do feel something for you. Something so strong that it's killing me! My father loved my mother so much and every day, even years after her death, I would see him sitting on the edge of his bed holding her picture and crying. Even after all the women who had come and gone out of his life, she was the one he couldn't let go of. And it scares me. I'm scared to love you like that because if I do, I may lose you like my father lost my mother. I tried so hard to fight my feelings for you, but I couldn't, and tonight, they became stronger than ever. I had to leave, Fiona, because I could already feel the pain of losing you."

*

Fiona

I stood there and listened to him expel his deepest fears. A man who was always in control. A man who proudly held his head up high. A man who was confident in everything he did, and a man who had been broken inside since the day his mother died. He was scared and he was afraid to love because of loss..

I slowly turned around and watched him crumble before my eyes. The sadness and despair that crossed his face was something that I'd never forget. Could I deal with this? With him? His fears? His insecurities? Of course I could, because I loved him. I slowly walked over to where he was standing, looking down at the floor as if he was ashamed, and took his hands in mine.

"Love is scary and it's okay to be afraid. There's always a risk when you love someone. But it's a risk worth taking, no matter how frightened you are. You told me yourself you're a risk taker. If you stop taking risks, you stop living life, and love is one of the most beautiful gifts given to us. It doesn't make you a weak person, Nathan. It makes you whole."

"I feel whole when I'm with you, Fiona." He squeezed my hands. "When you're not around me, I don't know—I feel lonely and I've never felt that way before. I—" He paused for a few moments.

"Keep going." I smiled.

"I can't stand not being with you. That night in Maine when I held you all night after we made love was the best feeling in the world. I never wanted to let you go. If I could freeze time, it would have been that moment I would have frozen forever. Then all that talk that Linden did about my parents brought back so many haunting memories of my father and his sadness. I tried so hard to push you out of my heart and my head, but I couldn't. As much as I wanted it to only be about sex with you, it wasn't. It was more. I got scared and I'm sorry. But now, having you here, I don't seem as scared anymore, and I think that we, me and you, need to," he took in a deep breath, "try to take our business relationship to a more personal level."

"I would like that. But only if you're ready." I smiled.

He brought his hand up to my face and our eyes locked on to each other's.

"Fiona, I—I…"

"Shh." I pressed my finger to his lips. "You don't need to say it yet. I already know."

His lips gave way to a small smile. "But what if I want to?"

"Take your time, Nathan. We're in this for the long haul. We have plenty of time. When you say it, I don't want you to be afraid. It'll just come out naturally without the double I's."

"You're crazy." He pulled me into him and held me tight against his chest.

"I know and I'll work on my crazy."

"Don't. I like your crazy and I don't ever want you to change. Crazy is who you are and who I fell in love with."

"Now I think you're crazy." I smiled as I broke our embrace.

"Maybe I am, but you know what they say about two peas in a pod." He grinned. "Stay with me tonight. Don't leave. Because if you do, I'm going with you. I want this weekend to be just the two of us. No work, no phones, no interruptions."

"I like that idea." I kissed his lips.

"How about spending the weekend on the yacht? Just us, the open water, and a big bed to have as much as sex in as we want."

"There's no other place I'd rather spend it."

Nathan softly ran the back of his hand down my cheek as he gazed into my eyes.

"I love you." He smiled.

"Are you sure?" I grinned.

"I've never been so sure about anything."

"I love you too, Nathan." Our lips softly touched.

Nathan

We spent a beautiful weekend on the yacht and now it was time to step back into reality. But somehow, even though we needed to get back to work, having her in my life still felt like a dream.

"I'll drop by the office later." I kissed her goodbye. "Will and I have a meeting."

"Okay." She smiled as she brushed her lips against mine again. "I love you."

"I love you too."

She left my home, and I watched as she climbed into her car and drove away. Spending the weekend with just her was without words. We had grown closer and I shared things with her that I never shared with anyone before. I was so in love with her and it felt good to be able to finally admit it.

"Is Miss Fiona around to stay?" Jason smirked as I climbed into the back of the limo.

"She sure is, Jason. She's not going anywhere and neither am I."

"I'm happy for you, Nathan, and it's about time."

I gave a small smile as he took off and drove me to the office. After Will and I had our meeting and I did some work that needed to be done, I headed over to Winslow Wines. When I walked into the office, I stopped and stared at the picture on the wall.

"What happened?" I asked Fiona, who was sitting behind her desk.

"The redhead had a run in with my heels." She smiled.

"Ah. I see." I chuckled.

Walking over to the picture, I took it down and walked it out to Josh's desk.

"Please discard this for me, Josh."

"It would be my pleasure."

Six months later

Fiona Rose Wine took off better than I had expected it to. She nailed it with the marketing and the wine was selling out faster than it could be made. She had worked her ass off with the launch and I couldn't have been more proud of her. As for Winslow Wines, production was going well and sales were up once again. We dumped Tobias Vineyards, just like Fiona said she would, and were now getting grapes from a family-owned vineyard in Sonoma Valley. I stayed out of Fiona's way because she was running the companies on her own just fine while I took care of my business at Carter Management Group.

Things between Fiona and me were perfect. This woman had drastically changed my life in more ways than one. Spending every day with her, whether it was at work, her wrapped up in my arms, or even just hanging out talking was the best part of my life. She was my number one priority now. Romance had quickly become my specialty and I spent every day making sure that I did at least one romantic thing for her. I had no doubt in my mind that we were going to spend the rest of our lives together.

I had arranged for a private dinner on the beach right outside my Malibu home. While Fiona was at the office, I had a beautiful canopy set up in the sand with a small round table, two chairs, white linens, and candles. I wanted to make this a special night for her.

"Hello," she answered.

"Hi, beautiful. I'm going to have Jason pick you up from the office and bring you to my house for dinner. I have a meeting that may run a little late."

"Sounds good, babe. I'll see you later."

"I love you, Fiona," I spoke softly.

"I love you too, Nathan."

CHAPTER 46

Fiona

Dinner with Nathan was exactly what I needed after the hellish day I was having. No matter what kind of day I had, he always made it better. Just being with him, wrapped in his arms was enough to make me forget everything. I was so in love with him and he made me incredibly happy.

Six o'clock rolled around and I climbed into the back of the limo.

"Hi, Jason." I sighed.

"Hello, Fiona. Rough day?"

"Just a bit." I smiled.

As I opened the door to Nathan's house, I set down my purse, kicked off my shoes, and walked into the kitchen for a glass of wine.

"Why hello there, beautiful." Nathan smiled as he walked in and wrapped his arms around me.

"Hi. I didn't know you were already home."

"I've only been for a few minutes. Come to the bedroom with me." He took hold of my hand.

"Can I pour a glass of wine first?"

"You can pour the whole bottle later. I have something for you."

"Oh?" I smiled.

When we reached his bedroom, I noticed a light beige maxi dress with spaghetti straps hanging from the closet door. Nathan walked over and handed it to me.

"I bought this for you to wear to dinner tonight."

"Nathan, it's beautiful."

"I'm glad you like it. Hurry up and change and I'll meet you in the living room."

"I thought we were staying in tonight?"

"We're just having dinner around the corner." He winked.

After changing into the dress and slipping on some sandals, I walked into the living room where Nathan was waiting for me and he held out his hand.

"You look gorgeous. Are you ready?"

"Let me just grab my purse."

"You won't need your purse."

I arched my brow at him and he smiled. "Trust me, Fiona."

Placing my hand in his, he led me out the patio door.

"What is going on?" I asked with curiosity.

"You'll see. Just follow me."

He led me through the gate and down to the beach where I saw a beautiful white canopy with a round table and two chairs sitting in the sand.

"Nathan. Oh my God. This is beautiful. Are we celebrating something?" I asked as I bit down on my bottom lip.

"No. I just thought this would be a nice change of pace."

"You are the most romantic man I know." I reached up and kissed his lips.

"Only for you, beautiful." He smiled.

He pulled out my chair for me and I sat down while he sat across from me. Beautifully lit candles graced the center of the table as well as the fine white china that sat upon it. A few moments later, a man walked over with a bottle of champagne and poured some into each glass.

"Dinner will be served shortly." The waiter smiled.

"Thank you." Nathan nodded. "Here's to us." He smiled and held up his glass.

"To us."

After having an elegant dinner, Nathan got up from his seat and held out his hand.

"The sun will be setting soon. Why don't we go and watch it?"

"Sounds nice." I placed my hand in his.

It was a beautiful night between the calm wind and the whispering sound of the waves that made their way to the shoreline.

"Hey, there's one of those aerial advertising banners. I was thinking about doing one of those for Fiona Rose Wines. I wonder what this one is advertising," I spoke as I stared into the sky.

"I don't know. I guess we'll have to wait and see."

As I watched the plane approach, I read out loud the banner that was floating through the sky.

"'Will you marry me?' Aw, someone is getting proposed to." I smiled as I looked around at the few people that were on the beach.

"Look, here comes another one," Nathan spoke.

I looked up and read the second one.

"'Fiona Winslow.'"

My heart was racing a mile a minute as I spoke my name. I looked at Nathan, who stood there with a wide grin across his face as he took both of my hands.

"You know I'm a businessman and I don't believe in entering into a merger agreement until I'm certain it's a lifetime investment. You, Fiona Winslow, are a lifetime investment, and I would love it if you'd do me the honor of entering into a merger agreement with me and become my wife?" He reached into his pocket, got down on one knee, and held up the most beautiful diamond ring I had ever seen. "Fiona Rose Winslow, will you marry me?"

I was shocked, stunned, and elated. Usually when I get like that, stupid falls out of my mouth.

"Are you sure I'm a lifetime investment?" I asked as tears filled my eyes.

"I've never been so sure of anything in my life." He grinned.

"Then yes, Nathan, I will marry you!" I placed my right hand over my mouth as he slipped the ring on my left finger. "Oh my God, I love you so much."

He stood up and our lips collided into a passionate kiss while our arms wrapped around each other.

"You have no idea how happy you've made me," he spoke as he broke our kiss and stared into my eyes.

"Hopefully as happy you've made me."

"I love you, Fiona, and I promise to love you and only you for the rest of my life."

"And I promise to love you and only you for the rest of my life," I spoke as the tears fell from my eyes.

"Let's go inside and celebrate our engagement." He smiled.

"You better hurry and get me back up to the house or else we'll be doing it right here in the sand because I'm ready to rip your clothes off right here, right now."

He chuckled as he picked me up. "I would love nothing more, but I don't think the people on the beach would appreciate it."

As he was carrying me to the bedroom, I heard my phone ring. He stopped and looked at me.

"Do you need to get that?"

"No. Whoever it is can wait." I brushed my lips against his.

A few seconds later, his phone rang.

"First your phone, then mine. I better check it. It might be important."

"Nothing is as important as making love." I grinned.

Again, my phone rang and so did his. Nathan sighed and set me down, pulling the phone from his pocket and answering it.

"Okay. Fiona and I are on our way."

"Really, Nathan? Where are we going?" I cocked my head and placed my hands on my hips.

"Lydia is in labor. That was Will and they're on their way to the hospital." He smiled.

"WHAT?! OH MY GOD!" I frantically ran, grabbed my phone and

purse, and headed to Nathan's car. "You're driving since Jason isn't here. We don't have time to waste!"

He held up his keys. "I know." He smirked.

CHAPTER 47

Fiona

"Come on, Nathan."

"Sweetheart, I can't help L.A. traffic."

"And I can't miss the birth of this baby. Lydia needs me." I pouted.

"You won't miss it. I promise." He grabbed my hand and brought it up to his lips.

We finally made it to the hospital and took the elevator up to the Labor and Delivery Unit, where Will was waiting for us.

"How is she?" I asked as he led us to her room.

"In pain. A lot of pain."

Stepping into the room, I ran to her side and grabbed hold of her hand.

"I'm here." I smiled.

"Oh God. Here's comes another—What is this?!" she screeched as she held up my hand.

"Nathan asked me to marry him, but that's not important right now. Focus."

"I am focusing on that gorgeous ring," she yelled.

The contraction subsided and she let out a deep breath.

"Congratulations! I'm so happy for both of you." She held out her other hand to Nathan.

Walking over, he took hold of it as Lydia squeezed both our hands tight.

"FUCK ME! This never stops!" she shouted.

Once her grip softened on our hands, Nathan kissed Lydia's forehead.

"Stay strong. I'm going to go wait in the waiting room."

It wasn't too much longer after Nathan left that Lydia's doctor walked in and told her it was time to push. I stood on one side of her while Will stood on the other. It was a struggle and there were a lot of obscenities thrown around, but she finally gave birth to a seven-pound six-ounce baby girl whom she named Finley.

I walked out into the waiting room, and Nathan stood up when he saw me.

"Well?"

"It's a girl."

"Wonderful." He smiled as he kissed me. "How are they doing?"

"They're both doing great."

Six Months Later

As I sat behind my desk looking over the quarterly reports for Winslow Wines, I smiled.

"What's that beautiful smile for?" Nathan asked as he glanced over at me.

"Take a look at this." I got up and handed him the reports.

He looked them over and then back up at me.

"You have successfully tripled the profits for Winslow Wines." He smiled.

"I sure did."

"Well then, I have a phone call to make."

"What if I don't want you to make that call?"

He got up from his chair and walked over to me.

"We had an agreement. If you tripled the profits within one year of our agreement, I would give you full control of your company back."

"Agreements are made to be broken, Nathan." I ran my finger down his chest. "I want you as my partner for as long as Winslow and Fiona Rose Wines are in business. I like having you around." I smirked.

"You only like having me around for the sex we have in the office."

"True." I shrugged. "But I also like knowing we're in this together. I'm a business woman, Nathan, and I don't believe in entering into merger agreements until I'm certain it's a lifetime investment, and I already knew when we entered into this agreement that it would be for a lifetime." I got down on one knee and grabbed hold of Nathan's hand. He chuckled. "Would you, Nathan Carter, do me the honor of staying my lifelong business partner here at Winslow and Fiona Rose Wines?"

"I would be honored, and I do." He smiled.

"Great." I stood up and wrapped my arms around his neck. "Now, what were you saying about sex?" I smirked.

Nathan

Fiona wanted a beach wedding and a beach wedding was what I gave her. She wasn't your traditional bride who wanted traditional things. It was a casual beach ceremony with a no shoes rule. No white runner. No tuxedos. Just the sand underneath our feet. I wore rolled up khaki pants and a long sleeve white cotton button-down shirt, untucked, of course.

I stood there as nerves took over me under the beautiful arch decorated with tulle, white calla lilies, and pink roses.

"You okay?" Will asked as he stood next to me as my best man.

"Yep. I'm good." I clasped my hands together.

"I never thought I'd see this day for you, Nathan. You make me proud, man." He smiled as he hooked his arm around me.

"And I never thought I'd see you playing daddy either."

"Yeah. Me neither, but I love that little girl and I love Lydia."

"So is there a wedding in your future?" I smirked.

"Yeah. I think so."

Fiona wouldn't tell me what music she picked to walk down the aisle to, which had me really curious. The wedding coordinator, Marybeth, walked up to me and spoke, "Are you ready, Nathan? Your bride is about to walk down the sand."

"I sure am." I smiled.

Suddenly, the song "Shake Senora" began to play and instantly my eyes diverted their attention to Lydia, who was holding Finley, and Josh dancing down the sand. I couldn't help but shake my head with a wide grin across my face. Once they took their place, Fiona followed behind, dancing down the sand in her white strapless, sweetheart neck, A-line wedding dress. Her hair was in an up-do with curls cascading down and she carried a bouquet of white calla lilies in her hand. She was the most beautiful woman in the world and she was all mine. She took my breath away. Once she danced her way down to me, I held out my hand and she placed hers in mine.

"You're crazy." I smiled.

"It kept you from crying, didn't it?" She winked. "And yes, but I'm your crazy."

"You sure are, beautiful."

After a short ceremony, the song played again and we danced our way up the sand and the guests followed behind, dancing along with us. After we posed for many wedding pictures, we met our guests in the white covered tent decorated with beautiful lights, flowers, and many elegantly decorated tables to accommodate over two hundred people. We ate, drank, and had great conversations with the people who celebrated our wedding with us. It was a magical night and one I would never forget.

It was time for our first dance as husband and wife. We stepped into the center of the tent and danced to "Beautiful World" by Aidan Hawken.

"I love you, Fiona Winslow Carter," I whispered as I held her close.

"I love you, Nathan Carter." She smiled as her lips brushed against mine.

And what a beautiful world it truly was. She had completed me in ways that I never knew existed and she turned my world upside down from the minute I saw her in the casino that one magical night. She was everything I wasn't looking for and she broke down my walls when I never thought they could break. She freed me from the imprisonment of fear that I held on to so tightly and I would spend the rest of my life thanking and loving her for it.

"We need to get out of here." I smiled. "I need to get you on our yacht and make love to you for the first time as your husband."

"Lead the way." Her grin grew wide.

We spent the first couple of days of our honeymoon on the yacht and then flew off to Belize on our private jet for two weeks, where we made the memories of a lifetime and our son, Nathan Carter II, also known as Nate. Two years later, in London, where we celebrated our two-year wedding anniversary, we made more memories of a lifetime and another baby. A girl, who we named London Rose Carter. Fiona thought the name fit since she was created there. I was not only a husband, but a father of two children. Two children who were my pride and joy and who would one day take over Carter Management Group and Winslow and Fiona Rose Wines. It certainly was a beautiful world and, every day, it became more beautiful.

THE ESCORT

CHAPTER 1

Brielle

I walked into the Warwick Hotel in my black stiletto heels and short black dress. My eyes were covered behind large round black sunglasses, which complemented my long dark wavy hair, and my lips, which were painted a cherry red. The lobby was quite busy this afternoon, and as I strolled up to the front desk, I was greeted pleasantly by Joseph, one of the clerks that had known me for the past five years.

"Good afternoon, Emmy." He began typing away at his computer. "Should I just charge the card that's on file?"

"Good afternoon, Joseph. Always." I smiled.

"Your key, Madame." He handed me the card. "Enjoy your stay."

I gave him a small smile as I took the elevator up to the thirtieth floor, slid my key card, and opened the door to the room I considered my second home: room 3010. After throwing my purse on the bed, I set my bag down and went into the bathroom to check myself one last time before my client arrived. There was a light knock at the door, and when I opened it, a man who was in his mid-forties and stood approximately five foot eight with short black hair and a light mustache nervously stood there.

"Hi, I'm Emmy. You must be Lawrence." I smiled.

"Nice to meet you, Emmy."

"Come in and make yourself comfortable." I gestured with my hand.

He stepped inside the room and looked around. His hands were fidgeting, and I could tell he was a nervous wreck.

"First time?" I asked to try and ease his nervousness.

"Yes." He turned and looked at me.

"How about a drink?" I asked as I walked over to the mini-bar.

"Sure. Got any bourbon?"

"Of course." I lightly smiled as I poured him a glass. "So, Lawrence, how do you like being a dentist?"

He answered my question and we made small talk. I always liked to have a conversation with my new clients first to ease into what was to come next. He sat on the edge of the bed while I slipped out of my dress. I could see the beads of sweat form on his forehead. I hoped to god this guy wasn't going to have a heart attack on me. I knelt down between his legs and softly brushed my lips against his, testing the waters, so to speak. He paid extra for kissing, so I needed to be sure he really wanted it. His hands nervously roamed to my breasts, which were covered by a black lace push-up bra.

"You're a very beautiful woman, Emmy."

"And you're a very sexy man, Lawrence," I spoke as my fingers unbuckled his belt.

After undoing his pants, I slid my hand down the front of them and grabbed hold of his semi-hard cock, stroking it softly and feeling it harden in my hand. He let out a moan and then grabbed my hand and pushed it away.

"I'm sorry. I'm so sorry. I don't think I can go through with this."

I sighed as I stood up and then sat down next to him, placing my hand on his thigh.

"Why don't you tell me what's going on at home that drove you to contact me in the first place?"

"I love my wife. I really do. We've been married for fifteen years and haven't had sex in over a year. She's always tired, never feeling well, the kids drive her crazy, and we grew apart. I hate that it happened to us. We're both so busy all the time between our jobs and the kids. Emmy, I'm starving for sex. A man can only take care of himself for so long. But despite all of our problems, I don't think I can cheat on her. I thought I could come here, have a fun time with you, and go home. But the reality is, we haven't done anything, and I already feel guilty."

"Listen, Lawrence. I love that you love your wife, and you should. You have a beautiful family and so many wonderful memories. What you need to do is reignite your passion with her. Take her on a date. Get someone to watch the kids and go away for a long weekend. I can guarantee that if you make her a priority and forget everything else for a minute, the two of you will be having sex again. You two just need to rediscover what it's like to be a couple in love. When was the last time you bought her flowers for absolutely no reason?"

"I don't know. Years, I guess."

"Then start there. When you leave here, stop at the florist, buy the prettiest flowers they have, take them home to her, and tell her how much you love her. Arrange for someone to watch the kids and take her to dinner. Don't tell her about it. Just do it."

He placed his hand on mine and gave it a gentle squeeze.

"Thank you, Emmy. I'm going to do just that. I'm sorry that I wasted your time."

"You didn't waste my time, Lawrence. Just remember that my fee is non-refundable."

"I know." He smiled as he stood up, reached into his wallet, and pulled out a hundred-dollar bill. "I know I already paid, but here's a little something extra for being so cool about all this."

I took the money from his hand, stood up, wrapped my arms around his neck, and kissed his cheek.

"Thank you. You're a good man, Lawrence, and your wife is very lucky to have you."

After he left the hotel room, I changed into a pair of ripped jeans, a long-sleeved black shirt, and my black Converse. Grabbing my phone, I sent a text message to Ben.

"I'm leaving the hotel in about five minutes."

"I'll be waiting, Brielle."

I grabbed my purse and my bag, put on my sunglasses, and walked out the door. Once I reached the lobby, I made my way to the front desk to check out.

"Let me guess, he couldn't go through with it?" Joseph smirked.

"No. He couldn't." I smiled.

"Enjoy the rest of your day, Emmy."

"You too, Joseph."

I walked out the doors of the lobby and climbed into the back of the sedan.

"That was quick." Ben smiled as he glanced back at me.

"He was feeling guilty. I sort of felt bad for the guy," I said as I took off my wig and pulled my long blonde hair back in a ponytail and placed a black Nike cap on.

I removed my green-colored contacts and placed them in their case as well as my false eyelashes. Taking the makeup remover wipes from my bag, I cleansed my face.

"Where to? Home?" Ben asked.

"No. I want to go to the shooting range for a while."

"You got it, boss."

Ben Riley had been my driver and one of my best friends for the past four years. He was a handsome guy who stood six foot four, black hair that he kept in a buzz cut, and a full beard and mustache that he always kept neatly trimmed. We met in a coffee shop when our coffees got switched. He grabbed mine and I grabbed his. Luckily, neither one of us had left yet. We exchanged coffees and got to talking. It turned out he had just lost his job as a driver to an influential family in New York City and was on the hunt for one. It just so happened that I had been thinking about hiring someone to drive me to and from my jobs. It was a win/win for both of us. He was a part-time artist who loved to paint and sculpt things. Unfortunately, what he did wasn't bringing in much money, so he depended on another part-time job to fill in the gap. It didn't take too long for us to become friends. He was my confidant and I could talk to him about anything.

Ben pulled up to the curb of the shooting range and I climbed out of the car.

"I'll only be about an hour," I said.

"I'll be waiting for you." He smiled.

I walked inside and saw Jimmy standing behind the counter.

"Hey, Jimmy."

"Hi, Brielle. Haven't seen you in a couple of weeks."

"Life, Jimmy. Life." I smiled as he reached under the counter and handed me my box.

Taking my lane, I put on my protective glasses and my earmuffs. Ejecting the magazine from my 9mm Glock 43 Caliber, I loaded it with bullets, disengaged the safety lever, aligned my eye with the target, and began firing.

"Damn, Brielle," Jimmy spoke. "God help anyone who pisses you off."

I gave him a smile as I stared at the six bullet holes that were perfect shots. After practicing for about an hour with moving targets, I unloaded my gun, packed up, and headed home.

"Have a good day, Jimmy. I'll see you next week."

"Looking forward to it, Brielle."

I'd been going to the shooting range to practice for the past five years. Being a twenty-seven-year-old woman alone in New York City and in my profession, I needed to protect myself. In case you haven't already figured it out, I'm an escort. Not just any escort, but a self-employed high-end escort. The men who acquired my services were generally the wealthy ones. Doctors, lawyers, hedge fund managers, CEOs, dentists, etc. You get the picture. Ninety percent of my clients were married. The other ten percent were those who had no interest in dating a woman but needed sex.

CHAPTER 2

*B*rielle

When I was growing up, I never in a million years thought that I would become an escort. It wasn't who I was. I was a bright and intelligent girl who got straight A's throughout school, graduated as class valedictorian, scored the highest number on the SATs, and got a full ride scholarship to any college I wanted. I didn't come from money. My mother was a single parent who worked two jobs, sometimes three, to try and make ends meet, and it still wasn't enough. We lived in a tiny one-bedroom apartment where my mother slept on the couch.

When I was eighteen, and right before I was scheduled to attend NYU, my mother was diagnosed with cancer and had to undergo many rounds of chemotherapy. Because she was so ill and missed a lot of work, she was fired and lost the shitty health insurance she had right before she was diagnosed. I had to put college on the back burner so I could get a job and take care of her. The problem was, the job I got waitressing didn't pay shit, even with the tips. She was getting further behind in her bills. Not only her everyday living expenses, but also the high medical bills that were rolling in. We were on the verge of getting evicted. I did the best I could, but it was never enough and we were both sinking fast.

One night, I ran into a woman named Marie who was having dinner with some people at the restaurant I worked at. When she stepped outside to have a cigarette, she saw me crying. She walked over and asked me if I was okay. I tried to play it off as if it were nothing, but she knew better. She got me to talk about my situation, and after she heard my story, she offered me some help. She told me how she was an escort and that she was getting ready to retire from it, but she didn't want to leave her clients high and dry. She said I was a beautiful woman and asked me if I'd be interested in trying it out. I'll never forget what she said.

"Listen, darling, you'll make more money in one month than you do for an entire year working at this place."

I didn't have a choice at the time, and I knew it would only be temporary until my mother and I could get back on our feet. She coached me, taught me the ropes, and when I was ready, she sent me some of her clients. I hated it, but I loved the money. These men paid me well, which allowed me to pay off my mother's medical bills and help us get back on our feet.

I escorted for two and a half years before I decided to get out of the business because of a man named Daniel. He was, or so I thought, the love of my life and swept me off my feet from the moment he looked at me. We dated for a month and trying to hide what I did for a living was difficult. As far as he was concerned, I worked as a home health aide with crazy hours. So I quit and ended up getting an office job as a receptionist working 9-5. We dated for about six months and I was happy. Happier than I'd ever been, until I got pregnant. The night I told him, he asked me if I was going to keep the baby. I was shocked that he would even ask such a question. When I told him yes, he hugged me and told me he was happy too. That same night, he went out to get us food and I never saw him again.

I gave birth to Stella when I was twenty-one years old. The company I worked for ended up closing its doors when I was on maternity leave. I took some time off looking for another job because

I didn't know what I was going to do with Stella, and needless to say, the little nest egg I had saved from my escorting days ran out quickly between living expenses, hospital bills, and schooling expenses.

As I sat holding her in my arms and stared down at her precious face, I knew I wanted to give her everything she deserved. She didn't ask to be born and she didn't deserve her father abandoning her. I wanted a better life for my daughter than what I had, so I knew what I had to do. Only this time, it would be different.

Once my mother went into remission and was cancer free, she got a job as a secretary in a real estate office. She worked the normal 9-5 hours and made barely enough to support herself and help me out. I could change that for her. So after having a long conversation, she agreed to quit and take care of Stella while I worked. This time around, my job wasn't the couple of hours here and there. Sometimes it consisted of two, maybe three-day weekends. But that was where I drew the line. I was never gone more than three days at a time. And when I came home, I didn't work for three days so I could spend all of my time with Stella.

My mother knew what I did for work. We never kept secrets from each other. And even though she didn't like me getting back into escorting, she knew I had to do what was best for Stella. Plus, she liked the money I paid her and the apartment I put her up in.

※

"Mommy." Stella smiled as she ran into my arms. Picking her up, I hugged her tight.

"Hello, baby. How was school?" I asked as I put her down.

"Fine."

"Just 'fine'?" I patted her head as we walked to the car.

"It was kind of boring. Hi, Ben." Her face lit up.

"Hello, little lady." He grinned.

We climbed into the back of the car and Ben shut the door and drove us home.

"Take your backpack to your room," I said as we stepped inside.

"What do you want for dinner?"

"Surprise me," she said as she took off down the hallway.

I walked to my office, where I found my friend and personal assistant, Sasha, sitting behind her desk.

"How did it go?" she asked as she looked up from her computer.

"He couldn't go through with it, so we just talked. I told him to take his wife on a date and buy her some flowers."

Sasha let out a laugh.

"I'll flag his account in case he wants to book you again," she said.

"Good idea, but I don't think he will."

"Mr. Willows called and booked you for next weekend. Friday-Sunday. He has an event in Texas he needs to attend. He's flying you out Friday morning and you'll be back Sunday night."

"Good. I like Texas." I smiled. "Are you staying for dinner?"

"No. Not tonight. I'm teaching yoga over at the studio. In fact," she glanced at her watch, "I better get going."

"Stella, Auntie Sasha is leaving. Come say goodbye," I shouted down the hallway.

Stella came running in and hugged Sasha goodbye.

"You're not staying for dinner?" Stella pouted.

"Not tonight, missy. I have a yoga class to teach."

Sasha Hathaway and I had been friends since junior high school. She was there for me when my mom was sick and she was there for me with Stella. Not only was she one of my best friends, she was my personal assistant and helped out with Stella from time to time. As far as anyone outside my little circle was concerned, I was a freelance marketing consultant. After Daniel left me, I took some college classes in marketing with the hopes of moving up in the company I had worked for. Little did I know they'd go under and it would become my perfect cover.

You can download The Escort by clicking the link below!

Amazon Universal Link: mybook.to/TheEscort

BOOKS BY SANDI LYNN

If you haven't already done so, please check out my other books. Escape from reality and into the world of romance. I'll take you on a journey of love, pain, heartache and happily ever afters.

Millionaires:

The Forever Series (Forever Black, Forever You, Forever Us, Being Julia, Collin, A Forever Christmas, A Forever Family)

Love, Lust & A Millionaire (Wyatt Brothers, Book 1)

Love, Lust & Liam (Wyatt Brothers, Book 2)

Lie Next To Me (A Millionaire's Love, Book 1)

When I Lie with You (A Millionaire's Love, Book 2)

Then You Happened (Happened Series, Book 1)

Then We Happened (Happened Series, Book 2)

His Proposed Deal

A Love Called Simon

The Seduction of Alex Parker

Something About Lorelei

One Night In London

The Exception

The Donor

A Beautiful Sight

The Negotiation

Defense

Playing The Millionaire

#Delete

Behind His Lies

Carter Grayson (Redemption Series, Book One)

Chase Calloway (Redemption Series, Book Two)

Jamieson Finn (Redemption Series, Book Three)

Damien Prescott (Redemption Series, Book Four)

The Interview: New York & Los Angeles Part 1

The Interview: New York & Los Angeles Part 2

One Night In Paris

Perfectly You

The Escort

The Ring

Elijah Wolfe

Second Chance Love:

Rewind

Remembering You

She Writes Love

Love In Between (Love Series, Book 1)

The Upside of Love (Love Series, Book 2)

Sports:

Lightning

ABOUT THE AUTHOR

Sandi Lynn is a *New York Times, USA Today* and *Wall Street Journal* bestselling author who spends all her days writing. She published her first novel, *Forever Black*, in February 2013 and hasn't stopped writing since. Her mission is to provide readers with romance novels that will whisk them away to another world and from the daily grind of life – one book at a time.

Be a part of my tribe and make sure to sign up for my newsletter so you don't miss a Sandi Lynn book again!

Newsletter
Website
Goodreads
Bookbub

Made in the USA
Middletown, DE
08 March 2023